Surrealism True Surrealism

True Surrealism True Surrealism True Surrealism
True Surrealism True Surrealism True Surrealism
True Surrealism True Surrealism True Surrealism
True Surrealism True Surrealism True Surrealism
True Surrealism True Surrealism True Surrealism
True Surrealism True Surrealism True Surrealism
True Surrealism True Surrealism True Surrealism

True
Surrealism

True Surrealism True Surrealism True Surrealism
True Surrealism True Surrealism True Surrealism
True Surrealism True Surrealism True Surrealism
True Surrealism True Surrealism True Surrealism
True Surrealism True Surrealism True Surrealism
True Surrealism True Surrealism True Surrealism
True Surrealism True Surrealism True Surrealism
True Surrealism True Surrealism True Surrealism
True Surrealism True Surrealism True Surrealism
True Surrealism True Surrealism True Surrealism
True Surrealism True Surrealism True Surrealism
True Surrealism True Surrealism True Surrealism
True Surrealism True Surrealism True Surrealism
True Surrealism True Surrealism True Surrealism
True Surrealism True Surrealism True Surrealism

Praise for Christopher Klim:

"Clearly establishes Klim as an author of considerable storytelling talent, *The Winners Circle* is perfect reading for those who enjoy the irony of satire."

—The Midwest Book Review

"While *Jesus Lives in Trenton* and *Everything Burns* sparked the desire for more, *The Winners Circle* is sure to cinch Klim's place among the top humor novelists of the day. He skillfully cuts the difficult task of blending humor and pathos, while telling a lively tale peopled with a variety of enjoyable characters."

—The Book Reporter

"Klim delivers clever and funny scenes, complemented by solid portraits of [the main characters] and an entertaining array of oddball secondary characters."

—Publishers Weekly

"Is there no genre this man can't write in? The answer is no. … Klim shines again… He has what it takes to make it onto *The New York Times* Bestseller List."

—The Word Museum

"In Klim's *Idiot!*, his finely honed images jump off the page."

—Duff Brenna, author of
The Law of Falling Bodies

"Mr. Klim has, quite simply, done it again… He returns to his home turf of New Jersey to put together an oddly poignant tale of wealth and emptiness, an extended parable about the nature of money in the United States and how it shapes and reshapes our interpersonal connections more than we might wish to guess or acknowledge. This novel is a song sung to the accompaniment of the Invisible Hand playing upon the harp of the heart…. and due to Mr. Klim's eminent skills of depiction (I like to think of him as a Hogarth of the word kingdom for the twenty-first century), we get to look at it from all angles and hear it in high-impact surround sound. There's even a little O.Henry-style twist further along the storyline, but I will not for the life of me reveal it—it knocked me on my ass with laughter and dismay. Not too many books do that to me, these days. *The Winners Circle* is eminent social commentary by a man who sees what he looks at. Keep 'em coming, Mr. Klim, keep 'em coming!"

—Jason Price Everett, *The Circle Magazine*

More Praise for Christopher Klim:

"Christopher Klim is that rare talent who brings characters and stories that resonate with the working class and excite the sensibilities of literary connoisseurs. Maybe he's the New Jersey reincarnation of John Steinbeck. More likely he's destined to become someone quite unique in the pantheon of American novelists."

–Robert Gover, author of *One Hundred Dollar Misunderstanding*

"Understated humor, lack of pretension lend this wry urban fable undeniable charm... Klim's lighthearted entertainment possesses genuine heart."

–*Booklist*

"Klim has a colorful past, and it comes to life in the pages of *Jesus Lives in Trenton*, which has an ear for realistic dialogue and an eye for city grit that would make Dashiell Hammett proud."

–*Philadelphia Weekly*

"*Jesus Lives in Trenton* is riotously funny. However it works on a deeper level as an allegory about man's thirst for grace in a chaotic world."

–*Time Off*

"*Idiot!* is a moving book. It makes you understand just what a few unkind words can do to a person."

– *MyShelf.com*

"*Jesus Lives in Trenton* is laden with laughs, insight and an overflowing abundance of literary skill. Amen."

–*The Boox Review*

"Anybody out there looking for a good read? Here's one for you: a down-to-earth What-if tale of a good marriage and what money—both the lack and surfeit of—can do to it. With credible, sympathetic characters and a well-wrought story well told, it starts like the shock of snakebite and reads on like a breeze. Like Christopher Klim's previous two novels, it's hard to put down till you're done. Christopher Klim's *The Winner's Circle* is a book that will offer good company for a long lonely journey or a lazy weekend on the beach, or anywhere!" **–Thomas E. Kennedy, International Editor, *StoryQuarterly*, author of *The Copenhagen Quartet***

Books by Christopher Klim

Fiction
Jesus Lives in Trenton
Everything Burns
The Winners Circle
Idiot!
True Surrealism

Nonfiction
*Write to Publish: Essentials for
the Modern Fiction & Memoir Market*

Juvenile
Firecracker Jones is on the Case

www.ChristopherKlim.com

True Surrealism

Christopher Klim

Hopewell Publications

Published by
Hopewell
Publications, LLC
PO Box 11, Titusville,
NJ 08560-0011
(609) 818-1049

info@HopePubs.com
www.HopePubs.com

International Standard Book Number: 9781933435244

Library of Congress Control Number: 2010937064

First Edition

Printed in the United States of America

Thanks to
Julie Brickman
Matt Ryan,
Crystal Wilkinson,
and Neela Vaswani.

More thanks to many others
from the Middle East to Asia and India
for valuable and generous information.

Stories from this collection were previously
published in *Down in the Dirt Magazine*,
Trajectory, *Webdelsol*, *Write to Publish*,
Writers on the Job, *Writers Notes*
Magazine, and *Yellow Mama*.

Table of Contents

True Surrealism

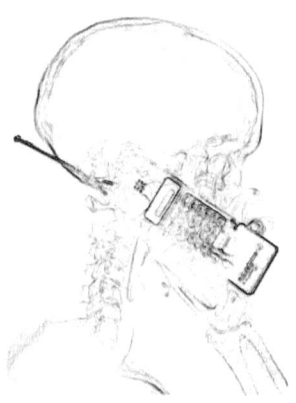

The smell of grease in the Horseshoe Diner was strong, like the residuals of every meal that had ever been cooked over its open griddle. I lingered in a corner booth near the window, speaking to my wife Ava on the cell phone. With as much free time as a corpse, I pondered past mistakes, but I kept the call short before she asked too many questions and revived the dying thoughts in my mind. A man was a sharp and useful tool, I thought, as long as he never paused to consider it.

"John, when are you coming home for dinner?" Ava asked.

"Same time as always." Beneath me, I felt the duct tape that crudely sealed the crack in the red vinyl cushion.

"Can you bring milk for the kids?"

"I have your note."

Thursday was milk day. To rescue the weekend for my vigilant wife, I must stop by the supermarket on my way home and pick up a gallon of milk. God forbid we should go without the comfort of milk or bread for a second. God forbid we should run short of anything, ever. And we never did. I had built a life where nothing failed expectations—bills were paid, heaters kept heating, roofs never leaked. We could be framed and shot by the Good

Housekeeping paparazzi, and they would never catch a brick out of place, a shrub overgrown, or our boys in shoes or pants a half size too small. Our life was perfect, until I ruined everything.

But no one knew, at least no one important to me, especially not Ava. I listened to her wonderful voice outline the mechanical details of her day. Not even the trains ran with such timing and luck—luck she didn't know was rapidly leaving town. I had lost my job at Smith & Wallace International Communications. Two years ago, I had been top salesman, before they siphoned off my commissions and out-sourced my accounts to a call center in Calcutta. At the time, I'd explained to Ava why my paychecks kept shrinking and the perks disappeared. No more lush dinners on the company. No luxurious cruises to the islands. Searching for coupons instead of vacation rentals, we downgraded our expectations from Peligrino to tap water. By settling Ava's fears, I held her terrifying worry-hives beneath the surface. She got into the leaner living, and then three weeks ago, SWIC laid me off me. I couldn't form the words in my mouth to tell Ava—me, John Gooden, the golden-tongued national sales leader of SWIC, Inc. My boys were too young to understand shifting markets and a father with overpriced skills. Unbeknownst to Ava, I spent my days weaving through crowds at job fairs like an undercover detective trying to make his mark. My credentials were camped on more Internet sites than cable television had sponsored programming. At my most desperate, I spoke to local fortunetellers about my prospects. Trying to divine my future seemed less difficult than processing the obvious facts, and keeping them both a secret was my new occupation.

"Don't worry, honey," I finally said. "I've got it covered."

I hung up with Ava and continued my morning ritual. My exit interview from SWIC included a cheery brochure that insisted I should maintain my daily routine. Boldly confident in its approach, it glossed over the part about separating me from the single act that defined my days. I was told to make appointments, keep schedules, and continue my regular habits, but all of this hinged on a regular paycheck. In western culture, it seemed that a man was defined by the pile of gold he created, and on Tuesday, my severance pay ran out. With my pot of gold shrinking, my best prospects lay over the horizon. God, I just didn't know where. Or when.

Which was why I became involved with psychics. I was not the type of guy who believed in the stars or premonitions. When people told me that they had lived past lives or received a signal from a dead aunt or a bunch of clouds arranged in a particular pattern, I tried not to laugh in their faces. However a few days ago, I discovered the alter ego of the universe. I was seated in the Horseshoe Diner, having coffee and a bran muffin that I would soon no longer be able to afford, when I spilled my troubles to Ruth, the diner's owner. Perched at a cash register with the Horseshoe's very first dollar taped to the front, she noticed that I wasn't leaving at 8:10 am every morning. I was searching the back of the newspaper and sometimes staring up at the talking heads on CNN who covered the same story ad nauseam. Ruth claimed that she'd seen this behavior before. At a glance, middle-aged unemployed men were dead giveaways.

"Yeah, I have no place to go," I said.

I almost admitted that I had a job with Edward Trask, the richest man in town, the benefactor of a dozen outlying towns and hundreds of charities, but that was only half the story. I wasn't even his advisor, accountant, or personal secretary. I worked a part-time job doing grunt work in his sculpture studio—not a gold star on my executive resume.

"How long have you been out of work?" Ruth looked as if she cut her hair with dull garden shears, a spiky creation that never laid flat.

"Three weeks." Although relieved to get it out in the open, I felt queer making my confession to a woman who only ever said "thanks honey" as I paid my tab.

"You ought to talk to Lucian. He has terrific insights."

"Like what?"

"Last year, when he noticed the chickens were dancing..."

"Chickens dancing?"

"He has a farm. When he saw the chickens, he predicted a twenty-two car pile-up on the interstate."

Already last week, in a tiled shack by the railroad station, I had visited a fortuneteller who laid Tarot cards in a pyramid on the table and then suddenly looked up and uttered, "There will be a man with sawdust on his boots." I liked that she didn't mince words, but frankly, if I was dabbling in the occult and shedding light on the unseen, I hoped for a little more information, such as the man with the sawdust boots held a generous employment contract in his hand. That information focused the beam a little tighter, but apparently psychics had their own lingo like everyone else. You had to pay them, not only to see the future, but also to explain what it was they were seeing.

"Who is this dancing chicken guy?" I asked, certain it was a wrong move, but with the right moves all dried up, the wrong moves were looking sexy.

"Lucian Cartier. He's famous in these parts."

Famous people in Centerville? It was amazing how we all lived now. You might be famous in your hometown and half the residents didn't know your name. I had been famous at SWIC for reciting our entire product line and rate sheet by memory, and no one at the Horseshoe Diner knew or cared. Hell, no one at SWIC cared anymore. When salaries and commissions were one tenth the cost in India, each salesman at the SWIC home office became famous in an infamous way.

"What does Lucian do exactly?" I asked.

"He reads the signs."

"Thanks for the tip." Preparing to leave, I knew better than to argue with someone's beliefs, especially if that someone served you food. You didn't joke with the person who fed you, and you didn't mock a person's faith. I had been joking all along, cruising really, never worried that the hand that fed me would bite my hands off to save a buck. And it wasn't just my ability to earn money. I no longer had hands for Ava, having lost that touch as well.

Ruth slipped me a note with directions for Lucian Cartier's farm. I knew who he was because I'd given him the middle finger last month when he'd blocked the road with his tractor. It had been the start of an awful week, and by the end of it, I had enough time on my hands to wait for him to plow an entire field.

As my Volvo pulled into the dirt tire ruts that split Lucian's acreage in two, I saw him near the barn dumping corn into a trough for the spring piglets. His boots were covered in mud and pieces of straw, which might resemble sawdust in a day or two, but I wasn't giving this one to the fortuneteller.

Lucian wore brown canvas overalls and an axe dangling from his belt. A rugged French Canadian, he had a bold face as if carved in Mount Rushmore—the unfinished side of Rushmore, with the pilot lines and weathering of years. He watched me rise from my car and walk toward the pigpen. With a glance, I knew that he recognized me from the road incident, but I got the feeling that he wasn't about to revisit the issue.

"I was expecting you," Lucian said.

Here we go again: another portentous psychic. I braced for a bizarre prediction to match the fortuneteller's sawdust boots.

"Ruth called me on the phone," he said.

I was relieved that conventional modes of communication still prevailed and Ruth hadn't signaled him via the brainwave highway. Trying to keep specific thoughts from my head, I focused only on an apology for the road incident. *Forgive me. Forgive me.*

"Did you think I read your mind?" Barely suppressing a smirk, Lucian dropped the feedbag and closed the gap between us. "I don't work like that."

"Then how do you work?"

"How does anybody?"

"We negotiate," I said, although I wasn't feeling on my game. For years, negotiations had been the key to my success in life and at work. Some salesmen made buddies of their prospects with gifts and favors. Others put on the hard sell and blew a good number of their chances. When people didn't see eye-to-eye, a good salesman needed to unravel the confusion and reach an understanding. I wondered if a person in Calcutta could do that over the phone, if a person who never set foot in the United States was able to traverse the ambitious, harried, underfed American mind. No matter how sophisticated or well documented the culture appears, some terrains required a native guide.

"I should have seen my layoff coming," I said aloud, "when they began building computer servers offshore."

"Last week, I had to order a replacement tractor part from Malaysia. The freight cost more than the part itself." Up close, Lucian's accent was more apparent. He spoke deeply, as if the words caught in the back of his throat.

"I just never figured they'd move the jobs offshore, too."

Lucian led me to the pasture where the sheep milled in clumps upon the uneven grass. With the henhouse upwind, the fetid odor of bird droppings, feathers, and who-knew-what-else reached my nose. Life on the farm, over the range, or in the woods never enticed my blood. I have resisted the notion of getting my hands dirty since finger painting in kindergarten. I've never planted a seed or chopped wood, even on a lark. If you asked me to dress a chicken, I might scan the L.L. Bean catalog for poultry cozies. Now I had to get my hands dirty, make magic out of the elements most foreign to me. I needed a desk, a phone, and a masthead on a business card that proclaimed me as an agent of an industry that mattered, that impacted real life, but I was an agent of free time, and everyone could get free time, if they wanted, when they wanted, even though they said they wanted and they really didn't.

Standing beneath the naked sun, we watched the sheep graze. Sheep have been historically depicted as puffy white clouds, skipping about the fields, but these looked like filthy mop rags in bad need of a rinse.

"You want to know how to proceed," he said.

Already knowing how to proceed, I wasn't ready to face that option. Years ago, I'd promised Ava to make the world stand still, to keep her schedules unaltered, and to keep her clockwork days intact, but with my world rotating out of control, I soon would be confessing my situation and setting her off on a frightful worry jag. No, I didn't need to proceed. Things needed to stay exactly as they had been before I joined the jobless ranks.

"But you don't know where to turn," Lucian continued. "The answer is all around us—in the rocks and trees, flowing in the wind."

"Can you help me?" I glanced at his overalls and large frame. Of course he couldn't help, and by the manner in which I asked the question, it was clear that I had little faith in his abilities. If I needed my hedges clipped or pets sheered, he was my man—but not for career advice, especially not for a glimpse of my days ahead.

"Arrière pensée," he whispered.

I didn't fully understand French but filed it away phonetically for the future. Any salesman worth his salt had a fast memory, remembering more than just names. He recorded a client's favorite food and drink. He recalled a client's birthday and if his wife was pregnant or his kids were graduating from school. He never wanted to be short a card to play later.

Lucian faced a hitching post where a chain dangled without a catch. "I used to have a goat—Trippy, a good girl, showed me many things."

"What happened to Trippy?"

As he pressed a hand to his neck, water formed in his eyes. "A hunk of potato. It was too big. She loved green Russets."

"She choked?"

"It was a bad day. The cows had been hind-stepping. I should have seen trouble coming."

By his solemn tone, I knew that we were entering a sales negotiation. Few people wanted to buy what was being offered to them. They wanted to release themselves of their problems and, in exchange, pay me for the service. A master at identifying a problem, I began parsing

Lucian's words to get at the core of his issues. "You said that Trippy showed you many things."

"They all do."

"The goats?"

"All the animals—they reveal how things will go and what to avoid, like when the cows lie down before a storm and the snakes slither to the creek for protection. But there was only one Trippy. She was the best, terrific insight."

That was exactly what Ruth from the diner had said. I let the information soak in. When negotiating, I needed to be careful not to rush or appear wanting, or else I might drive the deal away from the center of opportunity.

"The animals," Lucian said, "give me signs."

"Can another goat like her be found?"

"I don't know."

I gazed at the sheep as they herded themselves into the far end of the field. In the old days, before paper money rose to prominence and entirely destroyed the fair exchange system, people paid doctors with chickens and loaves of bread. They bartered for survival, often with the very items they needed to survive. I knew that Lucian required a goat—a goat like Trippy.

In the morning, like any day when the sun rose in the east, I awoke to the rustle of Ava in the kitchen downstairs. Hanging from the hook on the closet door was my gray pinstripe suit and a solid red tie. On the edge of the tub, a fresh towel sat beside a new bottle of shampoo. I heard Ava whispering to our sons Tim and Chad so as not to disturb me. It took a lot of patience and discipline to keep a pair of boys under ten years of age quiet, but without asking, this kingly treatment was mine—just a fringe benefit of my greatest negotiation.

Twenty years ago, I'd met Ava after she locked her keys in her car. She looked cute, tottering in circles on the pavement beside her green Chevy, sulking as a woman did when the odds were suddenly stacked against her. Her cocoa hair ruffled in the breeze like the feathers on a sparrow, and by instinct I moved in her direction to gather up her troubles. With a twisted coat hanger, I popped her car door open, watching her anxiety lift. A magnificent glow assumed her face, making me feel more powerful than I'd ever imagined.

We exchanged phone numbers, but it took more than a week for her to return my call and finally agree to meet. For months, it went like this—first not returning my calls and then jumping at my offer once we connected. I'd become enchanted by her gentle voice, her quiet focus, and the touch of her fingers as she held my face. Certainly she dated other men. I imagined her to be a sultry siren— full of secrets and avenues to explore and conquer. And I was jealous.

On a summer night, when the air smelled like hard rain and the blackbirds zipped through the twilight sky to seek shelter, I was heading through Ava's hometown and pulled into the local pharmacy parking lot for a soda. I spotted Ava coming through the automatic doors. At first she tried to turn back, but then realized that I was almost at her side and waited for my approach. A small bag dangled from her hands, and the clouds above resembled ebony fists of coal.

She looked agitated, like on the night we'd first met. As her feet shuffled on the sidewalk, her eyes appeared dilated and wary.

This only served to heighten my attraction.

"Ava!" I called.

Her left hand rose, covering her throat. She didn't speak.

"Where have you been?" I didn't mean just tonight but all the nights that she refused my calls. How could this sweet creature have a double life?

She took a step to pass, but I blocked her. Young and eager to force my will, I was foolhardy where today I am patient.

"John," she said softly, "please."

"What's the problem?" Only then did I notice the red marks climbing out of her sweater and up her neck, the worry-hives that have tortured her since childhood. When she was eleven, I later learned, they had become so fierce that her throat constricted and she nearly asphyxiated in the emergency room. But by now I was in love with her, and she could have shown me hideous scars or a fleshy stump and I would have swept her off her feet. Nothing was more perfect. I understood, like a man who had resigned himself to judgment, that this was an unavoidable fact.

With animal intensity, her eyes studied the cars coming and going in the lot. "I had to fill a prescription."

"Are you all right?"

"It will pass."

"No it won't." As the storm began, I kissed her. I didn't have the words to explain how nothing mattered from this point onward, and as the raindrops splattered upon her cheeks, she took my hand and pulled me toward her car. We stepped slowly at first and then ran beneath the opening sky.

"I can't handle changes," she said, as we jumped inside her Chevy.

"Who wants to change anything?" I leaned over and grabbed her waist with both hands. With her fingers, she held my face. We breathed heavily, and the windows fogged as if we'd become part of the rain.

"Make my world stand still," she pleaded, "and I will love you forever."

We made love in the parking lot of the Centerville Pharmacy. As we crawled like teenagers into the backseat of her Chevy, the rain blanketed the windshield, cleansing away the summer dust. Lightning cracked overhead, and I drank in flashes of her leopard-spotted skin. While kissing the welts on her chest and neck, I rubbed her spotted belly and arms as if to make them smooth.

"I can't bear our time apart," I said.

"Promise you'll hold the world still."

I wrapped my heart in an oath. "On my life."

Some days it seemed as if no time had passed from that night in the pharmacy parking lot and the dream was still pure. Ava maintained her end of the bargain, feathering the nest that I provided. When I'd sworn to quiet the storm in her life, I put down roots in Centerville and mapped out the focal point of Ava's world. Our home sat 1.5 miles from her mother and 1.7 miles from her sister in opposite directions. I kept a roof over our heads and the children in toys and chocolate. She cooked my favorite meals, making certain my attitude rose with the sun. Like the grid on the calendar, her days passed in lockstep, never hurried, predictable. If a man's worth in the western world was the gold that he acquired, then a woman's value was the gold that she consumed. I gathered treasure to the eye of the hurricane where my prize awaited—a woman of gentility, compassion, and a promise of love as solid and brilliant as the diamond slipped over her finger.

On my cell phone was two messages from Lucian. I hadn't told him about Ava or why it mattered that I kept my routine. He thought I just needed a job to pay the mortgage like everyone else.

"Ava?" Combing my hair, I looked into the mirror, but only a rough sense of my figure filled my eyes, the shadow and shape of me. I doubted that I resembled anything I once recognized. "Do you know where my black wingtips are?"

She spoke to me above the splashing of water in the kitchen sink. "Closing a deal, are we?"

Whenever I took an important client out to lunch, I wore my lucky wingtips. "I have an appointment." The truth teased at the underpinnings of every sentence.

"Your shoes are by the door. They needed polish. I'm sorry."

"Don't apologize."

"Excuse me?"

Coming to the railing, I overlooked the kitchen. Ava wrestled with a large pot in the sink, and as she wiped her face with the back of her hand, suds dropped to the rim of the sink. Her frame was short and sturdy but not the least unappealing. She easily handled bags of groceries or a load of wood for the firebox. Her physical strength belied her delicate center and an inability to manage crisis.

"You don't have to apologize to me," I said.

"Sorry, did I do something wrong?

"Please don't."

Ava cut the faucet and wiped her hands on her apron. Tim and Chad perked their ears, their faces peering up from splattered bowls of oatmeal. The view was stark: stacks of paperwork upon the counter, a broken light fixture that I'd ignored for months, Ava barefoot on the Tuscany tiles, and the boys oblivious to their mother's fragility. It had been a terrific twenty-year run, but was this the beginning of the end? Was this the point where the conversations became repetitious lies skirting the obvious? I saw the moment when a man determined to leave his family, when he could do nothing else, when he failed expectations and refused to proceed as less than what remained in the eyes of his wife and children. Deadly thin was the scrim between memory and reality. My family should never view the bottom of our coffers, never watch the taps of sustenance run dry. An essential part of me would rather break their hearts and whitewash my failure with their pain. But was there an image of me still worthy of viewing? No, they gazed upon the memory of someone they had known, the tool that had once worked and was now dull and useless.

"I received a call from Kyle McMahon yesterday." Slowly I entered the topic, wondering if Ava remembered his name.

"Oh?" Dropping her sights to the lunch bags for the boys, she stuffed them with sandwiches, apples, granola bars, and carrots cut into strips. It was more than they could eat in one day, even my two ravenous children.

"He asked for an updated resume," I said.

She stopped folding the edge of a paper bag, refusing to look up. "What's wrong with Smith & Wallace?"

"It wouldn't hurt to test the waters again."

"Has Kyle McMahon found anything local?"

So she did remember McMahon. He was a headhunter in Philadelphia. Last year, when I'd felt trouble brewing at SWIC, I called his office and circulated my resume. I took three interviews and received good offers—nice base salaries and expense accounts. In no time, I would top the stack rankings again, but each job required me to leave Centerville, and as I broached the subject, Ava dug in her heels. I thought I could see her hives rising as we spoke.

"Nothing local," I said, "not yet."

Moving nervously about the kitchen, Ava continued with the lunches. Her thin façade was slipping away. It always began with quick movements, and then she would drop a handful of forks or shatter a glass. Next, would come the tears that led to a breakdown.

I rushed downstairs. Almost leaping from the rafters, I took my precious bird in my arms. "No, no, no."

"What's wrong with him? Can't he find something local?"

There was nothing local. I was overqualified to sell all-season radials at the Quick Tire, and no one needed a salesman with a double-breasted suit and twenty years executive level experience to peddle footwear at Shoe Time. Condemned to dead-end, part-time employment, I kept it all hidden from Ava. "I told Kyle that. I told him to keep pressing."

"Changing your job is a big decision."

"I know, Ava. I don't take it lightly." I stroked her head.

"Everything has to be right."

"I understand."

The rest of the morning involved pacifying Ava. I quietly ate breakfast, laced up my shiny wingtips, and paused with my briefcase at the door to let her straighten my tie. At some point my home life had become a 1950's television drama, and I'd let it happen. It served me. Having Ava rotate as my nucleus affirmed that I'd always done well, even when I hadn't, because I had done well for her. Was it a crime to love her in this fashion? I recalled the faces of my children peering up from their bowls, curious about the drama unfolding between us, probably wondering if this was normal, their future. They were not tainted by any of this yet. If it took carrying ten times the burden, lifting the house upon my shoulders, I would do whatever it took to keep their world intact.

After leaving Ava and the charade of my daily commute, I skipped the Horseshoe Diner and reached Edward Trask's studio before 9 am. Each morning, Trask saw me change out of my suit and tie and into blue jeans and an old sweatshirt, and he never asked why. He was an eccentric sculptor, one of two filthy rich heirs to the Trask & Trask global fortune that was built upon solid robber baron achievements and extended through legitimate capitalist monopolism. In a studio that was embedded within a fifty-acre woodland preserve, Trask's mornings began with a glass of lukewarm Cabernet and a handful of chocolate-covered cherries. Often I found him asleep on the couch with a sleeve of saltines and a book of poetry, Whitman or Yeats typically, and I threw a blanket over him and another log in the Franklin stove. A man like this never questioned another. He was too absorbed in his own moments.

I had taken the job as Trask's shop steward—a glorified name for the sweeper of floors and a spare pair of hands whenever he called—because the work was more dignified than stocking grocery shelves and no one would stumble across my fallen status or, worse, report the news to Ava. Trask was famous for being rich, irascible, and religiously reclusive. Just to be left alone, he dumped thousands on local charities. Centerville boasted Trask playgrounds, the Trask Civic Center, a Trask women's shelter, and three Trask firehouses with engines nicknamed Ol'Traskie, Little Trasker, and so on. In a way Edward Trask, although never seen, was always with us. He was truly famous.

When I'd applied for the job, which amounted to a ten-minute conversation in the outer vestibule of his studio, he offered nine dollars per hour. He was pleased that I was not "a snot-nosed art student." When I joked that he should then double my pay, he replied, "OK, seventeen dollars cash, paid on Fridays." I didn't pass up the under-the-table offer, and there was another reason for taking the job. When I looked down, his boots were covered with sawdust. Chalk up one for the fortuneteller.

Doing little to earn my pay, Trask told me to place the mail unopened on his desk and never answer the phone. Occasionally I helped him direct a finished bronze statue onto a flatbed that was hitched to a vintage tractor, and then as I stood idly by the huge studio doors, I watched him cart something like the figure of a horse, ballet dancers, or a man with a drawn sword down a wooded trail to another building. Mostly I spent my days in quiet meditation, pulling his books on poetry and politics from the shelves. While the poets reflected the machinations of politics, the politicians reached for poetry to cover them up. Indeed people were capable of redefining the terms that governed their lives. It was best done quietly, art-fully, so no one noticed, but then again, when it inspired a reinvention of the rules, the best among them garnered outstanding praise. I had to be able to do this for my family. I must.

On the Friday of my second week, I cooked Trask a foil pack—bits of hamburger with succotash wrapped in aluminum foil with ketchup—as a late lunch atop the stove. I'd learned this recipe in the Boy Scouts, the apex of my culinary training. Seasoned with only pepper and salt, I feared that he might balk at the first taste, but instead he asked for the recipe to relay to his cook at the estate.

Trask stood with a foil pack in his open fist, digging with gusto at my Tenderfoot's delight. Regardless of the utter blandness of the grub served, a good cook fire brought men of all breeding together.

"Enjoying your time?" Trask was gray-skinned and very tall. He had about fifteen years on me, but many more years in knowledge and experience. Until you faced true intelligence, you never knew how much you didn't know.

"Do you like the job?" he asked.

What could I tell him? I had no health benefits, and my new career path was possibly worse than being unemployed. But in two weeks of near solitude with Trask, I'd made up my mind to take the first decent sales position that Kyle McMahon uncovered. Ava would have to deal with the change. Preparing for the shock, I planned to speak with her mother and sister in advance of a wicked panic attack, but I wouldn't pressure her to follow me out of town. I would see her on weekends and stay connected to her and the boys. Other men did it. I would do it. For this reason, for the time to think clearly about the future, I appreciated this job more than others I'd been offered. "Yes."

"Good," Trask said. "I might have use for you around the shop."

I shoved a forkful of lima beans in my mouth. What did he mean? I'd been there for two weeks, and he didn't have anything for me to do around the shop.

"I've got a good feeling about you," he said.

Here goes someone else with a feeling—a vibe. I didn't believe in vibes. No, I didn't believe him at all. I thought of the phrase that Lucian Cartier favored and mumbled it under my breath. "Aria Pensy."

"That's French," Trask said, a twinkle in his eye.

"I assumed." I was caught, reactive and embarrassed, face flushed over my steaming foil pack. Not knowing what I'd said, I considered an apology.

"John, you're trying to speak French."

Seeking silence to salvage the moment, I shrugged.

"Arrière pensée," he said. "Ah-ree-air pen-say. Do you know what it means?"

Certain it was an insult, I should've saved it to toss back in Lucian's face the next time he crowded my voicemail with talk of cattle movements and chicken formations. What had happened to my life?

"It's a wonderful expression," he said. "It's a doubt. It's an unstated doubt that keeps you from accepting something wholeheartedly. Arrière pensée."

Tapping the cell phone in my hip pocket, I excused myself to go check my messages. In the Communications Age, a timely phone call awaited—real or imagined—to extricate oneself from embarrassing moments.

Outside the studio, three whitetail deer milled beside a stand of paper birches. The deer scattered as I trod into the woods. The air was damp, and the forest smelled like budding fungi.

The cell reception on the preserve was lousy, and so I walked in circles, listening to the choppy signal. The first two messages were from Kyle McMahon—a pair of job prospects heating up—and the third message was a complaint from Lucian. I hadn't provided him with a new goat now that I "had a job." Twice, he mentioned Trippy in glowing terms. I wondered if he was capable of a reverse prediction, if he might erase my recent success no matter how small.

The final message was from Ava. In the little cell window, our home phone number flashed. It was two hours old. Walking deeper into the woods, I heard bits and pieces of Ava's voice. The broken-up playback didn't mask the fact that she sounded frantic. She'd intercepted a letter from SWIC, and she ranted about "terminated health benefits" and "re-career training." From there, she pieced together my trail of deception—five weeks of unemployment and days spent "God knows where." Far from the studio stove, a stiff breeze cut through me. I was exposed to the sun and the wind and my well crafted, neatly packed lies—all of it.

On the day Ava left the hospital, I moved into a one-room apartment above the Horseshoe Diner. Her mother and sister had assumed my position at home, sweeping me into the grave that they had dug for me. Her sister Eleanor wielded the biggest shovel. Whenever I visited my wife, Eleanor served up icy glares, sure to be poisoning Ava's mind in my absence. Eleanor was the one who'd rushed Ava to the hospital after she collapsed on the kitchen floor, when the boys wandered in from school and discovered their mother barely able to breathe, her face, neck, and arms resonating like the guts of a pomegranate exposed—an image that I'd never wanted my innocent sons to view in their lifetimes.

As I lay on the foldout couch and stared at the tiny apartment's spackled ceiling, evidence of the Horseshoe's late night crowd seeped through the floorboards: brewing coffee, easy laughter, sizzling French fries, pleas and bargains, midnight bacon and eggs. I couldn't sleep, instead processing the fragments fed to me earlier that day by the boys over the phone. "Mama's cleaning the piano again," Chad said. "I saw the checkbook under her pillow," Tim confessed. They waited for me to make sense of her behavior, but I traveled outside of her circle with no hope of rejoining. From her hospital bed in a medicated delirium, she'd asked me to "stop moving the walls in our house," and so I threw the basics into a suitcase and left home before she caught sight of me again.

Time passed like a leaky faucet, a slow tapping of water, an irremovable stain in the basin of my conscience. Money drifted out of our bank account to cover the mortgage and bills that marched toward our home without conscience. I cashed in my final stock option from SWIC. I traded in my Volvo for a used Kia. I sold my golf clubs and coin collection. My family resembled a hemorrhaging corporation, and fearing that economic repo-men might liquidate the business of my life, I imagined my wife and sons cast into the street. At my worst moments, I envisioned strangers in Calcutta drawing upon the equity of SWIC that I'd help to amass. Huge straws reached from overseas, sucking my bank account dry. Trapped in my isolated room, I clenched my fists and stifled my curses, resisting bitterness but not always. My unbridled words might blow the plaster clear.

At Trask's studio, I helped him raise the marble sculpture of an Old English sheepdog to the tractor's flatbed for hauling. The curls of shaggy hair were hardened in stone and jabbed at my palms, but I dealt with the suffering. Everything hurt inside and out. Through my joints and bones, a dull pain seemed to resonate without a center, without a prescriptive solution. Dreading a relapse of hives or worse, I lacked the courage to speak with Ava. I navigated my days, grasping for items that no longer remained at my disposal. Desolation came from inside the soul on out. My sentences ran incomplete, memories faded like signposts, and hopes disconnected from the future.

Tim told me that grandma and Aunt Eleanor were still helping out, and as much as I appreciated their assistance, I wanted to expel them from my home. I dreamed of carrying my wife and sons miles from Centerville, but as I closed in on a new job in a nearby state, I would be the only one who was relocating. My family, once as solid as Trask's statuary, had assumed a fragmented form.

The sheepdog statue shifted upon the flatbed, and for a moment, I thought I had gotten behind it, but as it started to roll on its base, it tipped forward. I tried to shoulder the load, but the weight was too great. The statue crashed upon the cement floor with a thunk and then squealed like the opening of a heavy jar lid. The head severed from the body, and several curls broke free.

Taking in the damage, neither of us spoke for a while.

"I'm sorry," I said.

Trask knelt beside the dog, examining the pieces. "It's not your fault."

"I couldn't hold it."

"I didn't have it cinched well enough."

"Sorry. I've been distracted lately."

"I've noticed." He wiped the stone dust from his hands, which coated his fingers like chalk, and rose to his feet. "Is everything OK?"

I stared at the big decapitated dog by my feet. If I'd fallen with it, I might have cushioned the blow, although it might have crushed me in the process. At least my life insurance policy was up-to-date. Surprisingly I still held value in certain markets. "Can it be fixed?"

"It doesn't matter. I'll recover the pieces in a new way."

"What will your client say?"

Trask shrugged. "Why don't you take the rest of the day off?"

"You need help cleaning up this mess."

"Go on." Trask spoke not with command, but with compassion toward a friend. He spent his days with still figures of bronze, marble, and granite, and I saw that he valued my company, as I did his. He knew of my trouble at home, but with all of his volumes of poetry and philosophy, he struggled for the words necessary in real life moments. Letting me off for the day constituted his best stab at demonstrating empathy.

"At least," I said, "let me call the client to explain how it happened. When things go bad at the plant, it's always the salesmen that make the calls. I have a lot of experience at apologizing."

"I bet you do." He shook his head. "There's no need for that."

The last reward I needed was a day off, so I could mill about town in my festering mood. I needed a job in Centerville and a path to Ava's heart. She wasn't a perfect woman, only the body of perfection in her flaws. Somewhere in her worrisome trail of thoughts, she must realize that I was only protecting her as I'd promised all those years ago. I cursed my fortune at SWIC, who shaved nickels off their balance sheet and ripped me from my family. Trask would never do that, but he didn't have a career for me either. Irony was no less cruel in the understanding.

After cleaning up the dead dog statue, I reheated my coffee in the microwave and checked my voice mail. I trod down the trail with my cell phone pressed to my ear and a steaming mug in the other hand. The air smelled of heather, and the birches budded for the onset of summer.

The big shed, where Trask carted his statuary, waited at the end of the path. I walked toward it in anticipation of a better cell signal. I'd never followed the tractor to the shed, much less been inside of the mysterious structure, and as I approached its red corrugated walls, I realized that it was further away and much larger than it appeared. It was a metal building, at least one hundred feet along one side. As temporary housing for Trask's finished sculptures, it seemed like overkill. Maybe he employed it as another studio or housed equipment necessary to finish his work. Even after scanning his sculpture primers on the bookshelf, there was much of statuary creation that I still needed to learn. The process fascinated me.

At the window, I cupped my eyes from the sun to steal a peek inside, but it was too dark to see. I tested the door to see if it opened, but pushing the door ajar did little to illuminate the view. Feeling along the wall, I hit the first switch that I found. A bank of fluorescent lights sparked to life across the ceiling.

I didn't believe my eyes. Dozens of statues in a myriad of materials and designs—people, animals, and scenes from history, nature, and fantasy—crowded the warehouse. Trask had used sheet metal, castings, and every conceivable method in my experience with sculpture, and although it was clear he had been experimenting for years, the eclectic works held one aspect in common: the fluid mind of a genius deep in thought.

Minutes passed, and my hand was still on the switch. *Good God, Trask never sells his work, not one statue.*

Returning to my apartment after work, I stared at the ceiling, listening to the plates and conversations shift below me. The lifeless figures in Trask's warehouse haunted me—three grey cats frozen to a tree, a rigid girl kneeling in prayer, and an eagle nailed to a tree limb. I thought about the psychics and fortunetellers that offered me snapshots of the future. They were like Trask, capturing the way we lived in the present and reaching for some sign of the future. The events in my life had brought me through Centerville, led me to Ava, and inspired me to build a world with a clock set for doomsday that I never imagined might arrive. *It's done. It's done. It's done.*

In the morning, I drove my Kia to the preserve and relocated each image in Trask's warehouse, just to see if I wasn't dreaming. I had hoped they weren't there and that I could drive to Ava and see that I hadn't destroyed our world together. In one of Trask's philosophy books, I had read that we dream in order to bridge the gap between our desires and reality, but there was no bridge from my reality to my desires, even when my desires had once been my reality. I breathed in the marble and granite dust—the scent of Trask's abandoned creations. Hoping for a return to the past was as crazy as hoping for Trask's statues to return to unchiseled stone. I knew what I had to do. I had to deal with the stones as they were.

Trask appeared in the doorway of his warehouse. "John?"

I figured he would be angry with me nosing around, but I was too ramped up to let his reaction impede my thoughts. With the desperation that measured my hours, I began to see the future. "What did you say once about Michelangelo?"

"Huh?"

"About the shape in the stone?"

"Oh, Michelangelo said the sculpture was already inside the stone. He had to release it."

"Are you surprised by your results?"

"Sometimes."

My mind shifted rapidly. "You don't have any clients, do you?"

He was taken aback by my directness. He glanced back at his studio. "I get so busy."

"This is a simple problem to solve."

"I was unaware I had a problem."

"Wouldn't you like more space in your warehouse?"

"Who wants this junk? Who wants to haul it out?"

Ideas caught fire in my mind. I considered selling Trask's statues on the side, putting together a color brochure, and making a tidy commission to supplement my lost income, but as I watched Trask stand before me, sipping on a glass of Pinot Noir, popping chocolate covered macadamia nuts into his mouth for breakfast, I realized that he desired nothing of the trivialities of business. I needed to sell his statues. He didn't. He needed more space in his warehouse, someone to keep him company and, once in a while, see that he ate real food. This would be a fulltime assignment.

If negotiating the shop steward's position had taken a few minutes, then returning to the studio and designing terms as Trask's Executive Statuary Sales Manager took only ten.

"Is that title OK?" I thought it would look great on business cards.

"Can I still call you John?" Trask asked.

Taking out a sheet of loose paper, I wrote down our agreement—salary, commissions, expenses, and family health benefits. "Is this good?"

"Whatever," Trask said.

I had recently told him that my oldest boy had taken to using that phrase as a catchall answer to anything, and loving the brevity, Trask made it his own.

"I think we ought to talk about vacation time too." I said.

"Whatever." Trask pulled a thirty-year-old bottle of cognac from the rack and cut the wax coating away from the cork. "Let's toast on it."

Trask was more than happy to have me dictate my requirements but mostly pleased that I was staying. I don't believe he cared if I sold a single damn statue, but I had goals in mind—one per month. Was it realistic? I doubted if I would equal my heights at SWIC. At least he wasn't about to fire me or export my position to Banga-lore in the middle of the night. Trask's father may have been a respected robber baron, Trask's brother might be a feared capitalist general, but Edward Trask was the antidote to his family ills.

With a better salary, I bought a replacement goat for Lucian. Loving the story about the goat shaman, Trask helped me pick out three young kids to send to Lucian's farm. There might be another Trippy in the lot. I had no idea. Trask treated the situation like an amusing anecdote, although I caught him staring into the goats' eyes as if to see if magic really existed. I think he worried that much of the outside world operated like my dealings with Lucian, which gave him further reason to be glad that I stayed to buffer him from it.

In the apartment above the Horseshoe, I dreamed a path back to Ava. I stuffed cash into envelopes and left them at her front door before sunrise, sometimes drawing a picture with my limited artistic skills. After reading Trask's copy of Dante's Inferno, I meditated on keeping a pure heart. With my torment made as real as Ava's hives, I had passed through the flame and awaited the next passage. What I desired was simple and without reproach: air, water, my children, my lover. Ava would understand the peace offering. She would know it was from me.

Ruth tried to offer more advice. Perched at the Horseshoe cash register, she fiddled with her permanent bad-hair-day hairdo. "You need to consult with Lucian again."

I nodded, thanking her twice, but I really wanted her to just top off my coffee cup. I wanted to hit the road and work with my hands and sometimes my head, to recreate the magic that appeared during the normal rhythm of the day. To make good trouble out of nothing. When I thought about the premonitions conjured by the psychics who came tangent to my life, I realized that they spoke about people and the things they might do or say, but I had been searching for events and signs, when I should have been seeking people—the company of trusted souls. All of my life, I saw, there were moments when I should have put my fate in the hands of someone else, if only for a moment, to let them weigh it, balance the product of my existence, register that it cut more than mere space on this planet.

During my fourth week apart from Ava, I placed the color brochure of Trask's statuary into a mailing envelope. The 8x10 glossy booklet held my business card with gold embossed lettering. To maintain the household expenses, I included another stack of twenties. Money was once again a token of my worth as a provider. If I could, I would stack twenty-dollar bills to the ceiling for her. I would build a sculpture of twenties if that returned Ava's favor. The green printed-paper held no other value for me, no other power over me.

Moments after my package arrived, Ava phoned my cell, but I let her speak to my voicemail. I recalled dating her twenty years ago, how she sat on my messages for days, how I did not understand her necessity to hide her dreaded hives from the man with whom she'd fallen in love, how I'd accepted her flaws yet allowed her to maintain the worst parts, allowed her to defer to me when she had managed without me for years.

At work, I took clients to lunch. They were shocked to see me in a three-piece suit and picking up the tab, but I quickly learned to play the artist game, wearing dark jeans and casual shirts with slogans like "Save the Whales" and "Guns Suck." Rumors circulated that I was Trask's starving apprentice, so I looked the other way when the lunch check arrived. The men and women across the table handled fortunes—large and small, private and public. They wanted a piece of Trask, typically without studying his catalogue for long. Many wanted showpieces for their corporate lawns and mansion foyers, but mostly they wanted to prove their ultimate worth in America. On the back of cocktail napkins, I wrote receipts for thousands of dollars worth of statuary, promising no particular delivery schedule. Most believed they had purchased art to order, when I might never empty Trask's warehouse of readymade statues.

When the fortuneteller called to follow up on her predictions, I told her about Trask's sawdust boots, but dared not inquire about my future again. A person could know too much. Trask had once revealed that beauty resided in the struggle of creation and that this was why he entertained little concern for selling the finished product. I did not want to see my future with Ava, or there would be no beauty in the process of rediscovery. Once, I had captured the future with her and etched it in stone like one of Trask's statues. No wonder it shattered when it tipped over.

Some nights, I waited in the parking lot of the Centerville Pharmacy, which had been taken over by a chain drugstore, and I hoped for Ava to approach me by luck and begin another glorious run. During the day, I looked out from the hill beside the warehouse, as Trask's welding sparks glowed in the studio down the trail. Studying the rooftops of Centerville from a distance, I wondered how many other people handled my burden, if their dreams had shattered into chards, if they emerged scarred and wiser. Other nights, I lay in bed, listening to Ava's messages, her voice puzzled, emboldened. I stuffed more cash in envelopes for my family and sent them into the universe like prayers. For the most part, I retained just enough money to pay the rent and purchase food and bare essentials. Two months had passed since I held my beloved bird in my arms.

On a Tuesday night, after a brief but hard summer rain that streaked the windows and sent dirt and trash washing through the gutters of Centerville, I received a call from Ava. She sounded quiet and determined. In prior weeks, the hurt and confusion had dissipated from her messages until no trace remained. Tonight, she held me live on the phone for the first time since March. An urgent tremor passed through me, but refusing to let my innate glibness rule the conversation, I used as few words as possible, conjuring the mystery that I had never before been for her. She threatened to get in the car and drive to my apartment. I said that I would like to see that and I would be waiting, but I did not say that this was the single call that I'd been longing to receive, the call where she defined the terms and she completed the negotiation.

I'm coming right over, she insisted.

I told her that I believed her.

Right now, she said.

Yes, I replied, right now.

The Final Ingredient

Nola J's Friday Specials
Sesame-Encrusted Salmon in a Wasabi-Saki Paste,
with New Zealand Mussels
Roasted Capon in a Tarragon-Chardonnay sauce,
with Spring Vegetables
Veal Nola with Cracked Crab and Tomatoes
Tri-Chocolate Mousse Cake

When the call came from prison, I was lecturing Faith MacPherson again. Waiters lingered by the salad prep, nibbling on the leftover spicy greens, and the dishwashers paused over sudsy piles of bone china, the steam moistening their hair. The staff believed I enjoyed criticizing Faith. I saw that look in their eyes, as if the show was on again. They thought I was insensitive and demanding, a real terror of a boss, but I loathed having to spell things out for her. I hoped that my example as a professional woman in the kitchen would be enough and that Faith might aspire to greatness on her own.

"The mousse cake was garnished with fruit." I studied her getup. Pink streaks accented her braided hair, and beneath her apron, she wore a flaming orange tube top. What could she possibly know about presentation and style? "It's supposed to be painted with cocoa and caramel sauce."

"Everyone does it like that." She spoke as if she'd reinvented the Caesar Salad. "I decided to go with sliced pineapple and kiwi —give it an island flair."

"This is Princeton, not an impromptu luau." I recalled her resume—excellent credentials, a woman to take under my wing. This business ground up women like discount chuck. By selecting her above more qualified male chefs, I'd taken an educated gamble.

"I thought the citrus complimented the rich flavors."

"The pairing of tart and sweet was reckless." I didn't have to sample her plate to know that the conflict would be World War III in my mouth.

"Can't we make adjustments?"

"Consistency is what matters." A diner saw magic emerge from the kitchen, but in reality a typical menu was set far in advance. I required skilled chefs who recreated the same illusion with pinpoint accuracy. "Customers want the Crème Brulee to appear exactly as the dozen times before. Do you understand? Exactly the same."

"That's a bore." To punctuate her impertinence, she blew her pink bangs away from her eyes.

I wanted to smack her. That was how my mother would have handled it. My mother was a woman who protected the limited space in her life with dramatic gestures. To mark her territory, she would have taken a step toward Faith and stared. This was my kitchen. The title on the engraved menus bore my name. When I was Faith's age, I had nearly perfect SAT scores and straight A's in college, but I wasn't saddled with being an impoverished single parent like my mother. I could've been a surgeon or an architect, but I wanted my vocation to be part of the everyday ritual, a constant reminder that the very best ingredients either achieved brilliance or were left to languish by lesser skills. For both my mother and me, there was victory in each stunning meal that I plated.

Ralph burst into the kitchen, holding the cordless phone from the front desk. "Ms. Jones?" He noticed the sluggish activity and then locked onto Faith and me near the large stainless steel doors to the cooler. Like everyone else, he knew that she was in trouble for the fiftieth time.

"You have a call." Ralph stepped softly, the soles of his Italian loafers sliding along the floor. His elocution was that of a practiced butler, even more so when exaggerating the point. "It seems *urgent*, but shall I inform him that you are *involved*?"

I snatched the phone away from him, ordering Faith to wait with a single glance. It was after ten o'clock and only three couples lingered in the dining room, chatting up alcohol-fueled nonsense over their desserts. If I wanted to create a scene, I could make the entire kitchen grind to a halt with a single command. "Hello?"

"Is this Nola Jones?" The caller's voice sounded gravelly, and he buried a cough.

"Yes."

"Thank God. I'm having an awful time with this dessert. It's coming out all wrong."

"Who is this?"

"Ben Kuppek. I cook at the prison."

"Trenton?" I figured he wanted food shipped for a prison function. *Oh, and just the thought of that.* "I only cater in-house."

"No, no. I need to make Zabaglione."

"It's simple: eggs, sugar, Marsala." I prepared to hang up and resume my argument.

Faith bit her nails, and I'd told her to stop doing that last week. Catching my glare, she stuffed her hands beneath her apron.

"Just whip it together over a low heat," I said.

"I'm getting it all wrong," Kuppek replied.

I brought my full attention to the caller. How strange it was that he wanted to make Zabaglione. He was an institutional cook, hovering over huge pots of chili which brewed in a kitchen with utensils resembling pitchforks and shovels, and the scent of ammonia cleanser flavoring every recipe. Deceivingly simple, Zabaglione was like carbonara and hollandaise, something a rookie took for granted and blew in grand fashion.

"Should I send you directions?" I asked.

Kuppek sighed a chef's sigh, as if he'd burnt the angel food tort or, in his case, the instant cake mix. An aspiring chef pleaded for assistance. Why didn't Faith ask for help? Even the waiters saw her struggle. She was either too prideful or, even worse, too lost to ask.

"Would you like me to demonstrate?"

"Could you?" He responded, a desperate lilt in his voice.

"It will be my pleasure."

"Armi said you were the only one."

"Who?"

"Hayden Armistice."

As if someone had thrown open the freezer at my back, I caught a sudden chill. I knew Armistice. He loved my Zabaglione. He was big money from Princeton and often made special, sophisticated orders. Requests like that turned me on, so I obliged whenever he posted a reservation. It had shocked me to learn that the courts had convicted him.

"Turns out he's got good taste," Kuppek said.

"The restaurant is closed on Monday. We do prep work for the week. You can come to my kitchen."

"That's cutting it close."

"What do you mean?"

"It's part of his last meal. He's set to go on Monday."

My eyes turned away from Faith. I pictured Armistice in his Burberry suit and gold cufflinks. He possessed perfect manners and a deep understanding of wine. It still didn't make sense that a man of his caliber should be put to death. At times it seemed that all the wrong people were cast aside like overripe fruit. "I didn't realize."

"I kind of wanted to get it right."

"It's the honorable thing." I often wondered how my meals finished the day. This one would be the last for Hayden Armistice. "Let me think. Weekends are crazy."

"I understand. I used to manage a little Italian joint on the freeway."

I let his comparison pass unmolested. "Tomorrow is a regular menu. Sunday is the Thompson Banquet. Everything will be on autopilot. I can show you then."

"Super. It will give me time to practice."

"You must practice."

After hanging up, I refocused on Faith, but the specter of Hayden Armistice pervaded my thoughts. On Monday, he would be spooning up my Zabaglione and then dying. I fought to recapture the thrust of my argument.

Faith leaned against the counter by the food processors, but as I returned the phone to Ralph, she slunk back to the spot in front of me. She reminded me of a cat I once owned. That animal harbored a lot of bad ideas, too. One involved scratching the hide on my leather couch, and so that the cat might reconsider its errors, I deposited the dull beast at the SPCA. It was my last pet.

"Fruit with cake," I said. The help had lost interest. Waiters charged through the door with trays of dirty dishes, depositing them near the sloppy water. They thought about counting their tips and hitting the road. They were probably glad that I had no words for them.

"It doesn't work?" Faith's confidence was waning.

"It cheapens the presentation. It's a shortcut."

"Shortcut?"

"Shortcuts are for diners." I hadn't intended to insult diners. I respected them. They mixed and matched a few dozen ingredients to fill a menu as long as a Michener novel. You could get almost anything you wanted in a diner, even if each meal tended to lump on the plate with similar color and consistency.

"I should've asked you first."

"You may ask, but the answer will likely be no." I thought that I might've been too harsh, but as she slid away, she stopped and looked back, her pink braids snapping around her head.

"Can I have Sunday off?" she asked.

I felt the punch sapped out of me. My hair was sweaty on my scalp, and my makeup felt grungy and exhausted. No question, I needed a spell in the sauna and a long, hot shower. "Sunday is the Thompson Banquet."

"I heard you say it was on autopilot."

Dividing my thoughts between who was in and who was out, Faith had just passed to the out list. She lacked the drive and intuition to uncover the masterpieces of her own design. Standing before me was a cold oven, an errant recipe. I dismissed her with a wave of my hand. "Work it out with Gerald."

Thompson Banquet
Moroccan Fish Soup Tangine Style
Smoked Salmon on Toast with Capers
Montasio Cheese Frico stuffed with Arugula
Angel Hair with Herb Pesto and Tomatoes
Baby Lamb Chops encrusted in Garlic and Herbs
Griddle-Crisped Chicken with Olives and Polenta
Assorted Pastries

On Sunday evening, I stood in Ben Kuppek's Chambersburg apartment, avoiding the madness of my kitchen. Dennis Thompson had been a patron of Nola J's since I opened the doors ten years ago at the age of twenty-seven. I was sure his banquet would roll without a hitch. I'd left the details to my other assistant, Gerald Basque. A quiet man, older than I, Gerald had scant flare but deft precision in the kitchen. A real wizard with the knife, he dressed meats better than any chef that I'd ever encountered. He deserved more of my attention. Soon he might be my only focus.

Taking out my cell phone, I dialed the restaurant. Earlier I had stopped at my kitchen, set up the appetizers, and finished the soup. I left the meats to the blade master, but before Gerald showed, I had to leave to meet Kuppek. It wasn't like Gerald to be late.

"Good evening, Nola J's." Recognizing my cell phone number on the caller ID, Ralph answered the phone with contrived dazzle.

"This is the chef," I said, our little joke. "Is my assistant in?"

"Yup, the pots are running over."

"How's Thompson?"

"Cheeks full of frico as we speak," he whispered. "Shall I go ask?"

I glanced at my watch, matching it against the tacky clock in Kuppek's undersized and poorly stocked kitchen. "Three courses down already?"

"They are licking the tablecloths tonight."

"Should I get back?"

"We can survive a night without you. You might consider asking Mr. Short Order out for a drink."

I scanned Kuppek as he moved about his narrow kitchen. He stood beside painted tiles of herbs and spices. The tarragon looked like sage, which resembled rosemary. At least they were green and buoyant, unlike Kuppek who appeared gray and weary from smoking too many cigarettes. How could he be a chef and dull his senses like that? As soon as I'd arrived, the first thing I'd asked him to do was to put out the cigarette... immediately.

"No such luck," I said to Ralph.

"No sparks?" Ralph quipped.

"I don't think our ingredients would blend well." My idea of the perfect man had impeccable taste and an evolved palate. There have been occasional pretenders and near misses, but in the end each man revealed his faulty sensibilities. I could spend the rest of my life waiting for the right pairing, and that would be fine.

"Too spicy?"

"Too stale." I watched Kuppek smile. His hair shined, thick and wet, permanently locked into a phased-out hairstyle. Holding on to a recipe that worked in the past but did not address contemporary tastes was a clear sign that you were finished. "Call me if there's trouble."

"Right-o captain."

A lesson in Zabaglione waited to be taught. I whisked the eggs and sugar in a double boiler, gently adding the Marsala to the fold. "Bring the temperature slowly to 160 degrees. Too fast, and you won't achieve maximum volume. Too hot and you'll curdle it. Understand?"

Impressed by my talent at the stove, Kuppek hung onto my words. He seemed to understand the process, but he held the whisk like a crowbar. Worse yet, he mixed unevenly, stopping at times. Again and again he demonstrated no inclination for the subtleties of fine cooking.

"Keep it going," I said encouragingly. "Are you friends with Armistice?"

"Friendly. Sometimes we sit after dinner. No one visits him on the row."

"What do you talk about?"

"Good food and European spa vacations. He knows a lot."

He frowned into the pot, watching the bubbles recede into the liquid. "I should've seen this coming. Usually it's shrimp cocktail and filet mignon. Killers don't often come from million dollar estates."

I assumed control of the whisk, vigorously attacking the mixture as we spoke. Dividing my mind between many tasks came naturally. To survive in the kitchen, you must handle three simultaneous operations at a minimum. "I can't believe they're executing him."

"I can."

I thought he sounded pitiless. Armistice was, after all, another human being. Before the liquid curdled, I reduced the flame. "He spared his dying wife more pain. Don't you think that shows compassion?"

Kuppek's head kicked back from the stove. "He's done it before."

"What do you mean?"

"He'd married another older women before this one. She was sickly like the second." Kuppek leered. "Both died unnaturally."

"You're joking." I admitted I hadn't closely followed the story. I still couldn't imagine the man I knew being anything other than polite, but then you never knew the true makeup of things until you reduced them to their essentials. That required patience and a watchful eye.

"Armi helped things along."

"How?"

"Poison. Slipped it into their medication."

"Unbelievable."

The conversation fizzled into the mechanics of the dessert, and after an hour and a half, I coaxed Kuppek into producing recognizable foam. He thanked me profusely, and I evacuated his ashtray apartment, relieved to find my silver Jaguar unharmed in the street.

I pressed the speed dial for the restaurant. "Where are we?"

"Assorted Pastries, Ma'am." Ralph spoke as if reciting the menu for the Queen of England. Sometimes, his routine got on my nerves.

"Success?"

"Four star, I'd say."

"Not five?"

"One complaint about fatty lamb chops."

I was mortified. "Fatty?"

"Yes."

"How did Gerald let that happen?"

"Gerald? Sunday is Faith's night."

"I thought they switched?"

"Who told you that? She came in late as always."

I hung up without saying good-bye. I felt like throttling Faith's neck until her pink braids turned a fuchsia shade of blue. It was all over, except for filling out her unemployment papers.

Monday
Restaurant Closed
Call for Reservations

I thrashed around my kitchen. When I was angry, I cooked with abandon. Dirty pots and cooking implements mounded everywhere, until the tools of my trade lay scattered about the counters like the inside of an army triage tent. As I pulverized the meats and vegetables in my path, the pungent spices and the feel of the blade in my hands soothed me. It restored sanity to a disheveled society, created beauty from chaos. A so-so meal rotted in the refrigerator for days, but a perfect meal lingered in the senses forever.

Veal shanks simmered in a pot of vegetables for Osso Buco. In a covered pan, Duck poached for Wednesday's confit. Over a low flame, a pot of seasoned trout soup and another with mushrooms and lentils melded together. The Osso Buco cast a scent of honeyed orange, and wafting from the trout soup was the smell of bouquet garni. I planned to set the soup aside. After a day or two, the soup would taste best.

46

As the weekly specials came together, the toxins in my veins began to subside. *I can run this place by myself. I don't need any help whatsoever.*

Faith entered the kitchen, just as the phone rang. I was tempted to fire her on the spot. I scanned her tie-dye outfit and beaded purse, conjuring little sympathy. *Clean out your closet and remove your wardrobe of knives immediately.*

"It's a disaster," Ben Kuppek said over the phone line. He sounded desperate again.

"Calm down. What's going on?"

"I can't get it. A dead man's waiting for dessert, and I can't pull it off."

"What does it look like?"

"Soup."

"It collapsed. Toss it and start over."

"Done that three times already." Kuppek coughed, then wheezed. The receiver fuzzed in my ear.

"The heat's too high."

"I know that, but any lower and the flame goes out."

I pictured the bulky institutional burner—great for boiling a pot of macaroni and cheese for hundreds of men. Hayden Armistice would never taste my Zabaglione again. It was a crime of its own. "I have a portable propane burner. You can bend candles over it without melting the wax."

"Thank God, you're an angel."

"I'll be there in thirty minutes."

After hanging up the phone, I stepped forward and stared at Faith. She stood at attention. Word had drifted back about the fatty lamb and my reaction. Her hands fidgeted with her purse strap. If she assumed the worst, she was correct.

"I have an emergency," I barked. "Watch everything."

I expected the dishes to be ruined by the time I returned.

Hayden Armistice's Last Meal

Oysters on the Half Shell

Pear Salad with Mixed Greens,
Walnuts, and Gorgonzola

Skate with Black Butter

Salmi of Squab

Zabaglione

I parked my Jaguar beside the mosaic on the prison's outer wall. A mural of joyous faces roamed beneath a helix of barbwire and watchtowers encased in bulletproof glass. A guard tilted his head in my direction. Smiling to assure him, I yanked my bag of instruments from the seat.

Ben Kuppek intercepted me at the gate. A guard patted me down, checked my bag, and escorted us to the galley. Retaining my composure, I tried not to focus on the electric gates, loaded weapons, and the creepiness of walking inside a place that any human being would want to escape. The prison smelled like loneliness, like a kitchen after midnight when everyone had left and I sat beside the cold burners with a glass of sherry. If I shifted too suddenly, I created an echo, the imprint of my existence bouncing back at me.

Brushing Ben aside, I set up the burner and lifted the sweet and savory foam in ten minutes. Crushed passion fruit fell from my spoon and into the airy mixture. Everything I employed—the whisk, double boiler, the very ingredients—came from my kitchen. No detail was left to chance.

As I exited the galley holding the Zabaglione, Hayden Armistice sat at one end of a long table. Kuppek had tried to take the fluted glass from my hands, but I stopped him. A matter of pride, this was my creation.

I set the dessert in front of Armistice, placing a silver spoon beside it on a linen napkin. Armistice's eyes were what I remembered, brushed metal in color. His mustache looked exquisitely groomed—black and peppered with gray. His clothes were prison issue denim, complete with stenciled name and number on the chest. While understanding the indignity of being poorly dressed, he would die in those clothes. I was glad I had packed the silver spoon and crystal.

"Miss Jones," he said, "or is it Ms. Jones."

"Ms. is fine."

"I was hoping you'd come. Please, sit."

By the swinging doors to the galley, Kuppek chatted with the guard. The pair seemed as unthreatened by Armistice as I was by Faith MacPherson. I pulled a plastic chair from the table and lowered myself into the seat.

Armistice dipped the spoon into the glass, retrieving a moderate portion of foam. I watched him slide the spoon into his mouth. His eyes fluttered ever so slightly behind the lids. The simplest ingredients, assembled with precise execution, conjured ecstasy on the palate.

"Marvelous," he said.

"Thank you." This was the experience that a chef rarely receives, witnessing the pure enjoyment of one's craft. Since cooking school, I had rarely captured the moment, but in this setting, it carried more gravity.

"I wish you had prepared the entire meal."

I wished I had as well. I should've suggested it. "No one asked."

For a second, the corners of his mouth turned down, and then lifted as he savored another spoonful. "The Zabaglione is treat enough."

"Thanks again."

"I regret not visiting your restaurant lately."

"I noticed you stopped coming around, before I heard about the trial." I went easily around the subject, but then I thought that he should control the dinner conversation. This one time, this one man, should be allowed to dominate the exchange.

"It was a taxing affair. My stomach couldn't handle more than crackers and broth."

"I understand."

"But that's behind me now." Setting the spoon on the table, he gazed across the dining hall. I wanted to turn around, although I knew there were only drab tables and monotonous walls behind me. A hunger filled his eyes, but if I dove into my repertoire of finest meals, I suspected that he would remain unsatisfied.

When he returned, his face appeared heavy. He carried baggage from wherever his mind had wandered. "Aren't you going to ask the question?"

"What question?" My first question would have been, how are you doing, how are you managing the monotony of confinement? But even that question no longer mattered.

"Everyone wants to know," he said, "but you are too refined to ask. I can tell by your cooking."

"I don't want to trouble you."

"But you are curious why I am here."

He was right. I too wanted to know why a man with everything went as far as he had. Studying the dead man, as Kuppek called him, I found him to be aloof and harmless. What actually lurked inside of him? What lurked inside all of us? Was it mere circumstance that kept us from unspeakable acts? Hayden Armistice had poisoned his wife. His previous wife had been exhumed and examined for traces of arsenic and morphine. The sobering facts caused me to shudder. I already knew the contents of Hayden's system at death: eggs, sugar, Marsala, and the lethal injections used to first sedate him, then bring him down.

"My wives were near their end," he said. "I tried to alleviate their suffering."

I held still. It was obvious that I was hearing his confession. With a dispassionate, steely eye, I caught myself sizing up Armistice. My analysis of situations had always been as clinical as a pathologist. While some chefs in training shied away from dressing a chicken or gutting a fish, I only looked for the perfect cut of meat. I envisioned it braising in a pan, glorified as a gourmet meal.

"But you cannot push things toward fruition," he said.

Like that errant cat I'd once owned, I pictured Faith roaming my kitchen without purpose. My expectations were for her to be someone else. Without question, I too had wanted the future to go differently, but if she was not a person of my design, then who was she?

"If I am guilty of anything," he said, "it is forcing the inevitable."

Chocolate Zabaglione
¼ cup whipping cream
½ cup semisweet chocolate
8 large egg yolks
¾ cup sugar
½ cup dry Marsala
pinch of salt

When I returned to the restaurant, the duck confit still simmered, but the soups and Osso Buco were set aside in good order. Lifting the plastic, I poked the veal shanks with a fork. They were tender and ripe with flavor, not overdone. The acid of the sauce had been reduced and successfully balanced. Part of me had wanted an easy excuse to dismiss Faith, to make problems disappear that were not entirely of her own doing.

I glanced at the clock edging toward midnight. Hayden Armistice's stay on Earth approached expiration. Kuppek had said that no one would be attending the execution except the family members of his former wives. Had I been the last sympathetic soul he saw?

Across the kitchen, Faith gathered the ingredients for Cocoa-Infused Sponge Cake. Most desserts were bought from a trusted Pennsylvania bakery, but to keep the menu honest, a few were still prepared on the premises. As she leaned over the counter, I noticed her pink hair restored to an even brown. I wondered if she had done this for me or for her next job interview.

She held an egg in the air, poised to crack it open, but as I covered the veal, she stopped in mid-motion. "Is it right?"

I tossed the fork in the dish bin, hearing it clank against the rigid steel. "The Osso Buco will be a hit on Wednesday."

"Am I working that night?" Her face was contorted, verging on tears.

I hoped she didn't crush the egg in her hand. "I admit I was going to fire you."

"I know. Everyone told me."

"You've disappointed me."

"I hear it in your voice... all of the time."

Her reply clarified my thoughts. Sometimes I didn't hear myself speak, but it was the noise of a driven and successful woman. Certainly I mowed down roadblocks, even if the roadblocks were other people. She had to learn that you couldn't regret every burnt flan, every collapsed soufflé. There were always other meals and occasions ahead. However, if patience was a spice, I had rarely added it to the recipe of my dealings with her.

"You have some bad habits, agreed," I said.

"I'm sorry I disappointed you." A tear ran down her cheek. "Before I came here, I'd read about you in the *New York Times*. I wanted to impress you."

"You stand somewhere between a cook and a chef. You must decide who you want to be."

"A chef like you. Should I pack up and leave?"

I saw how easily she was going to relent. *No, not the protégé I'd handpicked.* I'd fired better chefs for giving out free meals or moonlighting at other restaurants. One had waived a butcher's knife at me, but refused to follow me into the dining room and break from protocol and his innate respect for diners huddled over a gorgeous plate of food. Knowing a great chef when I see one, I still believed Faith had that capacity.

"Stop what you're doing," I said, "and I'll show you how to make Chocolate Zabaglione."

She rested the egg on the counter. It neither rolled off or away, waiting for the slightest force to influence its position. "But that recipe won't stand overnight?"

"When I'm through, you'll be able to repeat it for the Wednesday special."

With the back of her wrist, she wiped her eye, and then came to my side.

"Master that," I said, "and I'll teach you a few others."

Girl in Landscape

Mommy wants me to win. "How could you do this to me?" she says. "How could you?"

Her hands tremble, telling me not to speak. We are just offstage, and the other moms bustle in the green room, fluffing dresses, spit polishing high heels, and raking brushes through their daughters' hair. These moms—not unlike mothers I had in other lives—don't flinch at Mommy's razor tone. Yelling, shaking their daughters even, is merely a step on the path to winning. These mothers are no different than the fathers who holler along the sidelines of soccer matches, egging their sons into better images of themselves.

"It's step left, right, and two to the left—not one." Mommy wants to slap my face, but there are so many eyes around us, eyes like sponges soaking up our mistakes.

With the grace that was drilled into them, the pageant girls make detours around us in the corridor. This is my first show in Los Angeles, and for the most part, the other girls are sizing up my talents and forming opinions about my wardrobe. The event is not going well for me, and so the other girls are not threatened by anything Mommy and I do.

"How many times have we practiced?" Mommy says. "Huh?"

I can offer excuses, but that might increase her nasty tone. After all this is my fault. I know things about the past, and she is anxious, eager, wanting so much more here and now. The scrunch to her face summons lifetimes of disappointment, and I remember them all. There are so many different lives in my head that I can't always keep them straight. At night with the pillow wrapped around my face, I can almost hear and smell the past, places I'll never see in this lifetime. Whenever I share this secret with my best friend back in Tennessee, she stares with a fantastic expression. She thinks I'm making it up, says I don't appreciate the ribbons and trophies in my room, and as one hundred lives sweep through my memory, my thoughts go underground where they reach a wholeness of what I've always known. My current life, I realize, has never been better.

"What are you gonna say for yourself?" Mommy drops the hands that have been squeezing my shoulders and then clutches my wrist with as much spite. Pulling me beneath the glowing red exit sign, we enter the white-washed sunshine of Los Angeles. Oh, to disappear into the blinding sun, to be a part of the brilliant invisible land-scape. Ten minutes ago, I wanted to be outside, before the judges announced their opening scores. Never before have I dropped out of a pageant in the first round.

Every bone in my skull tells me that the car ride home is going to be terrible, but I want to get it over with. As Mommy backs the car out of the civic center lot, she almost crashes into a blue Honda. Its horn screams past like a speeding train.

Other moms are leaving, too, but most will stay to the end. Crowding the edge of the stage, they are enjoying the show. Some are only waiting to see who wins for Prettiest Hair and Prettiest Dress. Not Mommy. She's done with consolation prizes. We didn't move across the country just to watch another girl nab the top award. Jack Peltz, our manager and pageant coach, says that no one gets scouted in Tennessee; no one becomes a star in Knoxville. Brittany Spears came from Mississippi, I think. "If she didn't move west," Coach Jack said, "she'd be just another perky blonde combing the beach."

The mirrored buildings of LA toss a counterfeit sun back at us, and in the distance, the scrub-covered hills look as if no rain has passed in months, but what I most notice about LA is the competition. It is better, much better—the pricey clothes, the professional hairstyles, the polished routines, everything. Like little stars trapped beneath glass, the girls sparkle for attention. During the competition, Mommy leaned over to me and whispered, "All the easy points are gone."

As we drive away from the civic center, the highways around LA crawl like parking lots on escalators. Mommy barks over the cell phone with Coach Jack, reliving my pageant disaster. She details my misstep—getting a high heel caught in the hem of my dress—and the stumbling through my lines afterward. With one hand in the air, Mommy rolls her eyes and slowly shakes her head in exaggerated arcs, just like that ex-President's wife when she pretends the weight of the world is on her shoulders. Nothing is right, and even from where I sit, I can see that the dark roots in Mommy's blonde hair are bleeding from her scalp. We both need a "pick-me-up dye job."

Mommy tosses the cell phone on the seat by my hip. Her tone is dull, cooling off. "We've got a month to pull our act together."

"OK," I reply.

"We're just going to have to practice harder."

I am relieved that she's using the words "we" and "our" again. She is still with me, on my side. When she stays in the "you" too long, she raises her voice like an angry teakettle and the night gets strange. Crying, staring out the window of our dumb little apartment, she behaves as if she won't come back to us, that it will always be about me and my mistakes. I know it's the stress of her job and the car is making that noise again. When we first came to LA, it took two weeks for her to find a bank teller's position. On the last couple of days, we ate ketchup sandwiches and thinned the milk with water, but when I get my dance steps perfect, I'll be a winner again. All of Mommy's things will get fixed. We'll eat fresh berries and chocolate.

The car ashtray is empty. Mommy used the last of the change in the parking meter, but like the old days, I imagine it full of quarters and dimes, and I get this crazy idea of dropping change around town for people like us, people who need a few coins at the right moment. It won't take that much to help people out.

As we hit the off ramp, Mommy slams the steering wheel once and mumbles to herself. I appreciate the growing distance between the judges' table and our car, but Mommy is not ready to give up the show. Like an unlucky hand at Old Maid, she sorts through my mistakes, all different cards, never the one she needs. How much better off might Mommy be without me dragging her down?

◆

In this life, I've only ever lived in Tennessee and now California, but I dream of different places that I recall as clearly as the Knoxville Zoo or World's Fair Park. During the 1800s, I lived in England. The London sky was even darker during the day than the modern gray mornings in LA, but in London there were no cars. Horses and people choked the streets, and the smell of ripe fruit and fresh baked kidney pies punched the market air with promise and anticipation. As the crowd of grown-ups towered over me, I felt comfortable going unnoticed. If my luck broke right, I knew that soon I'd be looking down on everyone.

The Borough Market squirmed with activity, hardly a path to navigate, but remarkably, people seemed to know their destination. In the noise and calls for produce and price, Mum kept up a face for me, that ruddy complexion when the tears swelled up and ripened her cheeks like apples about to burst through their skins.

"Keep your chin up, luv," Mum said. She had cut my hair to look boyish. I didn't think anyone believed it, but surrounded by other kids in better circumstances than I, my lot didn't matter much. I looked the part, and no one questioned it. Sizing me up like a new pup, they pinched my ears and thumped my shoulders. A slender build and quiet demeanor was in demand. To demonstrate by agility, I shinnied up a lamppost like a rat. That was my tryout. I'd made the first cut.

"I'll spy on you," Mum said.

"Don't get your cheeks up," I said.

"Go on now. Do us proud."

I was partly happy about this choice, because a choice had to be made. Like kids have done through the centuries, my brothers went to the workhouses. I imagined generations of children dressed in baggy clothes, little men and women laboring over huge, thrashing textile machines. At times I saw myself watching over the children, helping them load the spindles faster. As the hideous noise rattled the windows and walls, kids roamed the factory floor with missing fingers and toes, without whole feet and hands, eaten up by those insatiable machines.

After Mum got some coin pressed in her palm, she left the Borough Market, and Master James took my charge. The sweep master was a stunted man with hair like a tangle of yarn, crushed in dirt and tucked beneath a ratty cap. From a short distance, I smelled soot on him, which was amazing with the coal stacks settling smog about us. I wasn't scared, mind you. I swear I wasn't. I only thought about impressing him and making Mum happy.

"All right," he said, "you ain't making keep by standing 'round."

"Keep," I learned, was a place to sleep and a daily meal, which was a big upgrade on account we'd been living on Toby Street since Pa died in the stables, actually sleeping on the cobblestones at night. When we got the news of Pa's accident, I 'member Mum throwing herself to the floor of the apartment we would be losing, because she knew what was to come of us without Pa's wage.

That first morning on my own, Master James took me on rounds, yammering on about chimneys. He bowed to his customers, yet whenever we were alone, he boasted like he owned the town. Certain enough, he charmed the kids to go about tasks. With one word, a child under his charge disappeared into the dark mouth of a fireplace both great and small. The sweeps scaled to the top of chimneys, scraping and collecting soot. It was all fascinating sport, but for me, independence was the main thing.

"I manage the crew," James said. "Do right by me or push off."

The crew consisted of boys and girls made to look like boys as I was. They were covered in more soot than Master James, making him look just plain dirty. What a sight the crew was coming down the street. You didn't need to be told what they did. I wanted to laugh but thought better of it.

At night we huddled in an off-shift flat on Denow Street, seven of us avoiding the drip in the ceiling, which splattered upon the dusty planks and spit up mud from the floor. Before dawn, the tanners would be in for our space, followed by another sleep shift before we returned. It was no problem getting out before the tanners. We smelled their stench coming up the steps, maybe even coming down the street.

Being the new sweep, the crew kept me at arm's length. I was a challenger, a threat to their standing. It was a prideful thing. A sweep might never be short of work. With ten thousand or more chimneys in London to scrape again and again, it was akin to arguing over stalks of hay.

One sweep, a young boy with a hooked nose, dabbed brine on those with bloodied knees or elbows peeking through their clothes. Biting back on the sting, the sweeps getting the brine only winced a bit. This was a tough lot of kids for certain, and so I knew my match.

The kid with the brine rag turned toward me. "These here chaps slipped the pipe."

I gathered he meant slipping inside a chimney while working, but I didn't reply. Speaking for a girl my age was usually a mistake, even more so with kids you didn't know, although this one sounded like he was using words put right in his mouth by Master James. All full'a smarts and high on himself.

"You'll slip the pipe once or twice," he said. "Every sweep does."

I took my bag—a used gunnysack for collecting the soot and ash—and draped it over my shoulders like the rest of the sweeps were doing. It made for a blanket quite right. Half the night I stared at the sweeps staring at me. They waited for a shiver or shake that betrayed my confidence, but I would never let them see that. I knew how pies got sliced. Like the world already knew how many mouths it could possibly feed, there was not enough pie for everyone. The weak kids and slow kids were served last. The fearful ones never got a scrap. I wasn't any of those types. With my fist all balled and tucked beneath my chin, I closed my eyes and thought about being the best damn sweep in London. I was a career girl now.

◆

Mommy wants to get me in "show shape." It's the morning after the LA pageant disaster, and to avoid any further trouble, I'm tiptoeing about our apartment. She pours a tall glass of "the drink" and sets it beside my cereal bowl. The glass is filled to the brim, thick and viscous, dripping on the folding kitchen table that we recovered from a downtown curb.

"The stage lights add ten pounds," she says.

"The drink" is supposed to be full of vitamins and minerals, but it tastes like liquid ash. It makes me pee all morning and then feel like an early nap. Occasionally I even throw up, which never concerns Mommy.

"Never be too proud," she says, "but walk as if you are."

I'm still in my pajamas—the blue nightgown with the white frill, the one she bought after I took the Tennessee Little Miss trophy. As she flips through some colorful paperwork on the table, I can spot the pageant guidelines from miles away. It's not so much the applications themselves. It's the way she looks at them—overflowing with expectations that I have to match. Every application has questions about activities, hobbies, and future goals. Future goals? Like every girl in the show, I want to take home the crown. Typically the pageant officials ask about my favorite TV show and any interesting facts. My most interesting fact is that my fingers are double-jointed and can curve backward like old broom straw, but Mommy never writes that down. She writes that CNN is my favorite show, making me sit through ten minutes of it before we leave for the pageant so I can recall something interesting for the judges. In each pageant application, there are diagrams of expected walking patterns on the stage, with marks for the places to pause and turn for the judges. We're like well-groomed pets in a dog show. Mommy has even joked that they ought to put us on leashes if they want us all to move the same way.

"We can do the Las Vegas tournament before Christmas," she says.

I nod my head. What will Christmas in LA look like with the palm trees dressed up for the holidays? I wonder if they skip Christmas in LA because it never snows. Does winter come to LA? Just the idea of not seeing snow again scares me. Over and over, this place seems stuck in the same idea. LA wants to be young and shiny forever.

"Drink up," Mommy says.

I take another gulp of her disgusting potion. After holding it in my mouth for what feels like a minute, I finally swallow, and my ears pop.

Mommy returns to her brochures and guidelines spread on the table like my homework. She plans to repair yesterday's defeat, but it feels like revenge, like we're always getting even with someone or something and we'll never catch up.

"Coach Jack swears that a pageant in Vegas is almost as good as Los Angeles," she says.

When I pour some of the drink into my empty cereal bowl, the sound causes her to glance in my direction.

"What are you doing?"

I don't think she's caught me. "Nothing."

She squints.

Flashing my best show smile, I wait until I can sneak more drink into the bowl. My entire world sits on the head of a pin.

◆

At night I recall beautiful Nepal, just before the life I am living today. It is so close to my current life that it sometimes overlaps with recent memories. Nepal was similar to Tennessee with rolling hills and green as far as the birds flew, but the Nepalese seemed happier with their hills. They ringed them with terraces and adorned them with lushly manicured crops—not like the endless chop-work of homes, shops, and pavement in Knoxville. Of course, LA is even worse in that respect with its smog, hard-faced buildings, and traffic going nowhere that I can tell. I always wonder about the land sealed below the California pavement, if it still has life.

In Nepal, we stayed in one place and worried about the hills. We feared that the ground would not yield enough rice or wheat. During the monsoons, we feared that landslides might sweep those crops and people into the valleys below. We feared too when the rains did not come. Like the daily rituals ingrained in our thoughts, these were the constant worries of my mother who was blind but walked the terraces in sandaled feet and handled the crops as well as any man with eyes.

When it rained, I planted sticks in the mud, forming a wall along one side of our house. I knew that I could not stop the land from shifting, but I gave no inch of soil without a fight. As raindrops pelted my head, I watched the mud glom to the upright sticks and the water rush about my boots. I was rooted to the earth. A single stick jammed deep into the soil was only a thread of protest against the elements, but a forest of sticks might turn back nature. I imagined a day when I could stop the mudslides, when I could stop the past from repeating.

In the hungry season, we wove raw jute for burlap and earned enough rupees to help us survive. The rough jute fibers slid through our hands, turning our skin into leather and filling our space with a musty scent. No one minded the labor, and as we worked, Bapa sang, stamping out the beat on the floor with my mother and brothers. Their songs of solace and peace echoed like lost promises through the generations.

Our two-room house sat on a hilltop near a spire like the nipple of a cat. The last time I saw home, the clouds sliced off the tops of the great mountains. My aunt had convinced my mother that there was work for me in Kathmandu. Young girls were sought for housework, helpers to the keepers of mansions in the cities. A long time ago, Aunt had "escaped the mountains," as she liked to say, to a finer part of the country, but I had only heard of such rich places. At first I could not believe they were speaking about me, but I was to bring pride to my family and wages that far exceeded my chances in the neighboring villages. Maybe we would not have to weave jute next winter. Maybe we would do it anyway.

When we reached Kathmandu, I entered the Durbar Square market where the pagodas climbed like disheveled stacks of books. Aunt guided me past the rug merchants who warmed their hands over ash pot fires. Open spice sacks were clustered beside the road, revealing all the colors of earth. The pungent odor of *dhulee achar* grabbed hold of my memory. A singular scent can be like a voice from the past, and in a flash, marketplaces throughout the centuries appeared to me and then the images disappeared along with the tiny ash pot cinders rising in the sky. I stutter-stepped, and even though the sun was strong and I was wearing the heavy stitches of my mountain clothes, I grew cold, as if the buildings drew the heat from my veins.

"Come, girl." Aunt tugged my arm.

I held my tongue. Ghosts were with me. Millions of people lived in Kathmandu, talking, laughing, and singing songs of want and value in the market. For certain, ghosts lived in that noise, but I felt only the ghosts of myself, and I saw madness that I could never fully explain.

"What is your trouble?" Aunt asked. "We're going to be late."

Stiffening her spine, Aunt pulled down on her coat. It was then that I noticed the fraying hem to her silk coat and the lines on her face. Often my mother spoke of Aunt's beauty and luck, but I only saw Aunt bracing against the slide.

"Come." Aunt yanked me by the wrist into a shop for a cup of *chia*, herbal tea made from the gelatinized seed. She waited until the *chia* flushed my face. "You are fragile like your mother."

Fragile was not a word that described my mother. Strength hid in her silence. Bapa laughed at the way my mother and I faced off, breathing in the other's reticence.

I stared at Aunt. During the whole trip to Kathmandu, she had barely looked me in the eye.

Scratching nervously at her arm, she bit her lip and then spoke. "Be stronger. You don't want to go blind like your mother, do you?"

After climbing four flights of stairs, we arrived at an apartment overlooking the square. I disliked the airless room except for its height above the street, but I was guided from the window and the curtain was drawn. In the corner of the room, a low-playing TV displayed the machinations of a pet competition. Dogs and cats were being forced through hoops, made to swim across pools of water, and dressed in silly outfits to resemble celebrities. They just wouldn't leave those poor animals alone. Hiding my face from the TV, I felt tears cloud my vision.

The apartment was owned by a woman whom I was told to address as *Didi*, elder sister. Didi was Indian, with purplish skin and markings upon her face. Beneath any light, we did not look like sisters.

"So fair and demure," Didi said.

"She lives in dirt," Aunt replied, scowling. "Sleeps in dirt, but she will clean up fine."

I wondered why Aunt referred to my family in those harsh terms, especially toward my mother who only spoke of her in praise and thanks, but Aunt was a person of knowledge that far exceeded my capacity to judge the world. Soon, the two faces of my aunt would merge into one.

When I was asked to leave the room, I heard tentative voices not unlike those in Durbar Square. Soon the haggling began. This was when and where my arrangements were finalized. Without a scale to measure my weight, without a question to evaluate my thoughts, the world had calculated my worth. There are no witnesses to crimes that are known by all.

For two days, I waited in a bedroom until a second girl arrived. Aunt had promised to return, but I knew that she was not coming back, that the face abandoning me in Kathmandu was Aunt's real face casting shadows over my future, my very soul. Plans were shifting, and meals were scant. Didi answered no questions.

The girl in my room whispered when we were alone. "Will the homes have television?"

Never having considered the possibility, I shrugged.

"Are we going together?" she asked. "Will there be other children?"

Who knew the answers?

On the third day, our questions changed. Riding in a bus teeming with families like migrating herds, Didi accompanied us over the Indian border and toward Mumbai. After the first three hours into the trip, Didi fed us water. Later she fed us rice bread from a roadside stand and complained about the price. At the border crossing, she fed us commands.

"No fuss," Didi said. "My clients demand respectful girls."

We nodded in unison.

"You were handpicked," Didi said. "Smile at the border. ... Remember, I am your Didi."

Later I wondered how much I colluded with my fate, not a shred of protest, but by then it was already too late. I could plant a forest of sticks in the dirt and never hold back the course of my fate or the will of my anger.

"Prepare for great changes," Didi said. "Mumbai is a big and expanding city. ... Your families have afforded you an enormous opportunity."

Hopeful assignments were promised, wealthy clients who would teach us to read and write and eventually drive a car. Fantastic thoughts. My heart sung with excitement. With hands clasped together, we pledged to work hard and earn our client's respect. For the price of our labor, our families anticipated great joy. We were both twelve years old.

◆

Mommy says not to talk to strangers.

Near the Forum Shops at Caesar's Palace in Las Vegas, the spiral elevators circle the ruins of ancient Rome. I like the giant reproduction of Michelangelo's *David*. He is naked and unafraid. As if I am to be embarrassed, Mommy ushers me past the statue, but David is a rock star, and I don't see the point of being shy over the facts. His collarbones sweep to the sides like scaffolding. His arms dangle like great, clawed machines, and that thing between his legs is perfect, although I've never seen one this close.

Mommy leaves me behind and enters the bar with a man whom I have to call "Uncle Britt." She and I cannot afford a room at the hotel that is hosting the pageant, but it's no trouble. Mommy is in "show shape," wearing her tight black dress, ruby lipstick, and her re-blonded hair pinned up with rhinestone combs. Strutting the floor without actually strutting, she can win whenever she wants. It is a pity there isn't a pageant she can enter.

Inside one of the jewelry shops, I pretend that I can afford whatever I want. I am wearing my one good dress from Talbots, and the salesgirl shows me a ruby bracelet. It's two thousand dollars. Slyly, I don't ask to see the ten thousand dollar diamond necklace or the two hundred dollar knockoff. That will show that I cannot afford either. The salesgirl sneers at me, but she must be careful not to insult me. So many children have more money than God and they don't even know it. By chance, she cannot insult a rich man's daughter. With the bracelet draped over my wrist, I hold it to the light without clasping it, as if I will not let such a cheap piece of junk encircle my wrist, just like Mommy does.

"The stones are too uneven," I say. I know the salesgirl hates me, but my clothes are better than hers. She is dressed like the women who Mommy calls "hookers," the women roaming the strip outside of the fancy hotels.

Among the ruins of Atlantis, I sit and order a diet coke with lemon. I take out the Gameboy that I'd won in the Little Miss pageant and select a lunch that Mommy will not normally let me eat from the kids' menu—macaroni and cheese, too many carbohydrates. If Mommy sees my plate, it will cost me one of her super-sized special drinks or a pint of orange juice mixed with Metamucil, which is like drinking sawdust.

I let the waitress know Mommy is coming after her spa treatment that she really isn't getting at the moment. Sideways glances shoot my way, but as a veteran pageant queen, I can fool the President of the United States. Besides, just like she did for this dress, Mommy will eventually find a way to pay for my food.

Two hours after lunch, Britt finds me near the sculpture of Poseidon with his pitchfork stabbing the air. I finally get a close look at Britt. He's got that smile that most of Mommy's men get. Patiently, doing my part of our travel routine, I wait for him to invite me up to the hotel room. I've never seen Mommy fill out a guest registration form or check luggage with a hotel bellhop. With a shiny silver credit card, Britt pays my meal tab and leaves a generous tip in cash.

He takes me up a swift elevator. Thankfully, his hotel suite has a small outer lounge with a television set. No having to wander the halls and lobbies while Mommy entertains Uncle Britt. He seems nice. Thank God, he doesn't try to make small talk, try to be my temporary daddy. I simply cannot stand fatherly advice from a total stranger, but if Britt stays quiet, I will not mind seeing him hang around for a while, although I know he won't.

Hanging on the back of a barstool is my blue taffeta pageant dress covered in plastic. There's a couch for me to curl on, and Mommy has left out a blanket and pillow. Flicking on the TV, I watched the late-night cartoons that I'm not supposed to watch at home. Except for the extra blood and jokes about sex that I'm not supposed to understand, I don't see the problem. The jokes about violence—shooting, stabbing, beating people up—are just cartoons of the news.

In the next room, Mommy is laughing and doing things to make Britt happy. I hear her champagne laugh. It scents the air like candy hairspray. She has a red wine laugh, which is sadder and smells like moldy leaves, and a vodka laugh, which is sour and can get scary if the fun of it fades too early. I know all of her laughs. I've experienced each of them secondhand.

◆

"Each chimney is different," Master James said, as we walked far from our usual London district. "It's got character from the man who bricked it. Got bents and turns too. Character."

It was only us that morning, the way I preferred. James was a good master. If I was moving too slow up the pipe, he never stuck needles in my feet. There were masters who did this and worse. Not Master James. He never lit a straw fire beneath me, never tried to make me climb faster than necessary. I was his champ, he said.

"How much money I got, James?" I knew not to ask him unless we were alone. He was different then. I could call him "James," and he might thump my shoulder. I think he forgot I was a girl, and being one of the boys wasn't all bad.

"You're gonna do your pa right proud," James said.

I figured I was doing Pa right proud already. He was watching me from heaven. Maybe he had a pint of bitters or a big box of chocolates up there. "You think I could see my money?" I asked.

"Don't have it on me." He stopped in front of a long iron fence that was higher than us both stacked up. "You think I'd be taking very good care of your stash walking 'round the streets with it?"

For a while, I studied his face, on account he could be lying, drinking it up like other sweep masters did or just plain shaving it until it was gone. I hoped Mum saw the payments she was promised. "I suppose you know best."

"You suppose quite right then." Tugging a string of dark licorice from his jacket pocket, he snapped off an end for me.

I chewed the sweet candy, looking at the fancy houses about us. In South London, the chimneys rose majestic-like, not like the chimneys near Denow Street that crowded the roofs like cannons aimed at the sky. In front of us, the chimney beyond the iron gates towered seventy feet in the air, a double barrel with three sets of trim on top and out-courses ringed in white. It stood beside a three-story mansion, which made a proper house for a man with plenty of silver. As if we had all the time we wanted, James and I drank in the glory of it.

"Ah, that's a fine one." James turned to me. "Told them all 'bout you."

"What'd you say?"

"Said you climbed faster and higher than smoke."

The accomplishment ran all through me. I knew the other sweeps were getting jealous. I never slowed down and never got bogged down with the cough neither.

"Well, sucking smoke's for the lazy boys," I said.

On account the help never goes through the front door, the housekeeper led us around back. It was funny. I always saw the dining rooms, bedrooms, and the private stuff in the end. You had to get the sweeps to the fireplaces, you know. Whether we used the front door, back door, or climbed through an open window, we got to see the whole house. I saw fancy wood floors and brilliant chandeliers. There were high-back chairs and gorgeous, fluffy couches covered in flowery material. To sleep on a couch that soft, I'd give up my little toe. The foyer had windows in the ceiling made of stained glass. You couldn't figure it—windows in the ceiling!

Round back, the kitchen fireplace was a huge cast iron devil that opened like a burnt out cave.

"This here first," James said.

Without too much stalling, I checked the lashing on my slippers. I no longer owned a pair of shoes on account that slippers climbed better. After purchasing my slippers in the market, James shaved the cost from my pay just like he did for my keep. It was fair, I suppose. "A man needs his tools," James had said, which was funny 'cause I wasn't a man or even a boy, but I hoped to have the pleasure in some life.

The bricks were still warm from the breakfast fire, which was good on account of the chill outside. Bracing my feet on one side of the pipe and wedging my shoulders along the other, I did the crab shimmy that the crew had taught me. This tore at the skin along my neck and elbows, at least the places not yet scabbed over. I never complained. Worse jobs existed, like rat catcher or scavenger. I saw the mud larks wading in the stinking Thames at low tide. Those kids harvested bits of coal, rope, and stuff like that to sell for scrap. There were even worse jobs. The sweeps that didn't cut it might wind up as nightmen, emptying privies about town, which made the mud larks' labor smell sweet just thinking about it. Other kids got set up as tanner's apprentices, which had to be foul on account of the smell alone—outdid the privy work. And girls? Girls did things they shouldn't do at any time in their lives. Worse jobs for certain.

"Get on, now." James' voice echoed up the chimney. The housekeeper had left him alone with the cook, and if I knew James, he was convincing her to unlock the cabinet with the cooking spirits. "I require my nips," he liked to say.

I shimmied upward, occasionally slipping on soot cakes and grease but holding my position, ever aware of the danger. The hole of daylight above me widened, setting clearer forms upon the firebricks leading toward the roof. In every climb, there was a point where a sweep fought off his or her nerves. It was a place halfway up and halfway down, too far to slide without breaking an ankle and too far from the top to call it done. In a sixty-foot chimney, I might hang for minutes before the master called up wondering about me. Neither up nor down, I braced myself just right. Held between the fresh air above and the common earth below, the dust of a thousand fires burned in my nostrils, but for the world, I believed that I could just stay in this half dark place like I once was inside my mum, all full of hope and promise and none of the daily bother. Then a cloud passed over that little window of daylight and I knew I got to get to it, and so I climbed. With the fury of fire, I climbed, and I forgot about fear and falling and soot and grime. I climbed like I was part of the pipe and right into daylight and clean air like I've never tasted it before.

Pulling myself clear of the pipe, I draped my feet over the edge. The city spread out like Mum's quilt bed-covering—the patchwork of it, richness and slums mixed together, bits of toss and bits of keepsake pretending to be unaware of the other, but sewn together in close fashion. How beautiful the city looked from up top. I saw the Palace, that white beauty, and started wondering if the Queen had chimneys, if I would get to go up Ma'am's pipes one day. I'd passed the Palace once and didn't recall seeing any smoke. Was there something else that kept her warm? Maybe the servants—because everyone knew Ma'am had countless servants—trapped the smoke and carried it to another part of town. You know, Ma'am could have people like that—people who gathered the smoke inside big balloons. Once from a rooftop, I saw a hot air balloon over the Thames and just knew it was filled with that special kind of smoke, like smoke from the Palace. It would explain a lot of things that didn't make right sense. When I got my fortune from James, I planned to hire a balloon and fly over the rooftops. I aimed to lean over the basket and drop a pence for the mud larks. Wouldn't that be something when they found a real coin in the mud?

Up top, high and free, that was how I felt. The rainbow-necked pigeons sat on the roofline, bathing in the sun, setting off a multi-colored display upon the moist roof tiles. As long as the pigeons hung near me, I had stained glass of my own. A rooftop was the place to be in the morning, the dew misting off the slate, the city small enough to grab with both hands. Me and the birds shared a feeling up top. Freedom was the word. Master James talked of it. "Providence." I wasn't sure what he meant, but it sounded like a place where you could do what you want.

I swore those birds thought I could fly, but I would have to put off proving it for the time being. I needed to start scraping and collecting ash on down to the kitchen. Catching my breath, I let the sun soak in and work its way to the bone. It would take another couple of minutes for James to start his mad rattling with the chain upon the chimney.

When I decided to get to it, I pivoted on my backside toward the hole, and the top two bricks gave way on account the mortar crown wasn't in such good condition. As a rush of adrenaline tanned my hide, I heard the clatter of bricks upon the slate roof. I feared my error: Master James lashing me for the damage, shaving my fortune for the repair.

The birds lifted from the roof, as I sunk toward the mouth of that big kitchen chimney. Rotten luck. I had slipped the pipe merely seated above it and minding my own business. Head first, I dropped into the darkness, clutching a handful of mortar and grit. I lost my grip, gouging my arm on the jagged edge.

Every part of me, each farthing of my fortune, knew what I had done. I was falling. Bird wings fluttered over the hole that sucked me in. I didn't call out. Fear, panic, and laughter tumbled in my stomach.

As I scratched at the walls, the creosote-slimed firebricks slipped past my fingertips. I clawed deeper, gathering the thousand fires beneath my fingernails. The morning sunlight closed above me, creating a dark place where gut reactions led my thoughts. Accelerating, I touched off the firebricks, twisting my body to wedge my shoulders and brace my feet.

This stopped me halfway down the pipe. My heart pumped, and my breaths drew tight and short. I was pleased over my lucky break, but my legs—twisted in a frustrating position—didn't budge, and the back of my head was pressed against the grime. My chin dug into my chest. So fast was the fall, like the crew had warned: *There will be no thinking when you slip the pipe.*

Unable to shift my head or knees from the chimney wall or my arm from behind my back, I was stuck. Something felt not right about my neck, and now that I found the words, I couldn't call for James. I couldn't even mumble, much less breathe. Any movement—a simple wiggle or shimmy—might suffice to open my throat and give me a taste of the ash that swirled about my face, the ash that flavored my breaths and darkened my fair skin.

Letting my muscles fall slack, I tried to complete the drop and expel my body from the black throat of this rich man's chimney, no matter what form I took on the landing. I was in a part of London that I'd never been during my short life with shorter time remaining, miles away from Mum's soft bed in the flat that we no longer shared. Might I truly be nowhere and missed by no one, surrounded by hundreds yet deadly alone?

The square of daylight above me faded faster than day. I watched the firebrick grow blacker than black, and as the warm pipe cradled me, I dreamt of Mum and Pa and those balloons over the Thames.

◆

Mommy says I'm in a dead heat with the girl on stage.

Aware of this for some time, I am studying the girl's routine for the talent portion of the competition, the last event before the prizes. I can tap dance and sing, but she does gymnastics and that dance with the ribbon. Girls and gymnastics create a killer combination.

This girl is good. Shifting and zooming, her ribbons swirl like a tunnel. It is as if she has more than one ribbon going at once, and without delay, the crowd socks her with praise.

My turn, I give a perfect song and dance routine. It's my 1940's "bring it on home" medley. At three points during my allotted time, the steps and tempo change, and I nail each transition. Three of the five judges are nodding, but I keep myself from staring, focusing on my steps. I've never done this routine so well, and the crowd sweeps applause over me, but when I am onstage, it's hard to tell if they love me as much as the other girl. Still the thunder of applause is scary and wonderful, totally Disney.

As if the judges have made up their minds in advance, the results come swiftly. I want to tell them how much we need this win, how much I need it. But the world has another bad joke to play, never running short of rotten cards to deal. By exactly one point out of one hundred total, the other girl wins the trophy: 98 to 97 points. I am second place. *I am second. Second.*

Mommy's face burns as if she's actually caught fire. I can tell she wants to rush the judges' table, wants to crumble up the puny savings bond I won and toss it back at them, but somehow she contains herself. She flashes on me instead. "Couldn't you try harder?"

I don't speak. I never speak at this point. There will be no business cards pressed in Mommy's palm, no calls from advertising agents and talent reps. The other girl has the limelight, and it will last as long as she remains cuter and prettier than everyone else.

"Haven't I done enough for you?" Mommy asks without really asking. "Don't I work for this too?"

A look emerges in her face. It's the one I hate, the one where the skin scrunches between her eyes. A word fist forms in her mouth. This time she doesn't need to throw it, but it comes out in slow motion, landing right on the mark. Unable to get out of the way, I recognize that the scrunched skin between her eyes is a mirror image of her knuckle prints in my chest—the imprint of her word fist crushing my heart.

"You are just a goddamned loser," Mommy says. "Worthless."

There are many things I might say, some she will never understand, or at least she pretends not to understand me or know who I really am. Partly, what she says is true. I am worthless to her and will never satisfy her. And I will never understand what she truly wants.

As I turn, handfuls of blue taffeta are clutched in my fists. Without being fully aware of my steps, I run outside the showroom and into the hall. The fountains in the lobby spew water like fire hoses, and the mirrors divide my image one hundred different ways. None of this is important. None of this is real. I forget that this is the best life I've ever lived and that I should be grateful.

◆

Walking toward my destiny in Mumbai seemed longer than it stretched in measure, longer than the path up my mountain home in Nepal. I never went to a proper school, so tell me how my journey differed from the Trail of Tears across the Mississippi River, the Armenian Great Calamity into Syria, or the train ride to Dachau?

Mumbaikars called my price in rupees, although I did not realize at first that the call was for me. I spotted hungry, taunting faces composed of a passion that I did not yet understand. Didi had brought us to a townhouse with a red light that incessantly glowed outside the door. Here I learned that the sum total of my worth was 70,000 rupees, a mere $1,500 American. This was the amount negotiated by my aunt betrayer, who was blinder than my mother. If I earned ten times my price, I swore to spend every coin on making my aunt see, making her look up from her life and lay eyes upon me.

"Is this the place where we will live?" My companion's voice betrayed all of the fear that I locked inside. Hardly breathing, I vowed to never speak and reveal my thoughts.

The street outside our new home appeared to be constructed of dust. People rattled and hammered about the city during the day, even worse at night. Garbage went unattended, and rats scurried through the gutters like unkempt pets. In the mountains, I lived lower, closer to the land, and there was nothing as fragile and unsettled as this place of grime and stench. This was a street of hunters who were always searching.

I shared a room with seven other girls. Heavy curtains separated us for privacy. With barely enough space for seven beds and passage for the clients to maneuver, I memorized the steps: five along the bed, ten to the towels for washing, thirteen to the bathroom. These were the exact dimensions of my life, a small and tight place with faded flowery wallpaper and tornadoes of plaster upon the ceiling. With all day to study my environment and the changes in people, the boundaries of my spirit grew tighter and tighter.

In the box of our lives, we learned to be respectful and pliant. This was strictly enforced. On the first night in my new home, lonely and alone, I tapped the floor to Bapa's weaving song. Softly, I thought, until *gharwali*, the house owner, whipped me with a cane for disturbing the visitors. He bruised the back of my calves and the bottoms of feet—the places normally unseen by clients. Biting back on the pain, I learned to walk without groaning—more emotion to swallow deep.

I did not learn *gharwali*'s name, and he never asked for mine. I was *tsukri*, child of debt. Tsukri entertained fifteen clients on a slow day, forty on weekends and holidays. For a favored young Neapli girl, eager Mumbaikars paid a good price, and almost as if apologizing in advance of their deeds, some whispered their appreciation in the low light. Tsukri did things unimaginable on the quiet mountains of Nepal, unforgivable by her family, impossible for my mother's dark eyes to bear. She touched the men, made them happy, and took them inside her body in any place they desired.

Yes, I learned something of desire, the way it rose like hunger and shifted like a sudden storm off the mountain ranges. Because of desire, you can see only what is in front of you. Desire had no limits but fit in the box of my life.

However, not all men were content with their want. There were men who shied away at first approach and men who breathed like dogs. A few were tender, and some who brought more anger than I saw in the wild. If they did not appreciate my fake smile, they struck me until I showed real tears. Some clients, I convinced to use condoms, but *gharwali* instructed us not to insist and so it hardly ever happened. I was in pain most days that I worked, which was every day of the year. For the first two years, I did not leave my box but to shower and then only within *gharwali*'s sight or the grasp of his husky guards who might do anything because there were no crimes in a place where everyone was a criminal.

Stolen from me was the quiet and peace of mind that came from a simple day on the cliffs. On warm afternoons, I used to draw water from the well and bathe beneath the valley sun. I was not ashamed of my nakedness. I did not believe it was different or more necessary than others', but the harmony of Nepal was no longer real to tsukri, only hopeful forbidden revenge against my aunt lingered. Impossible thoughts kept my heart beating, trailing away from an irretrievable past. Not for any time did I forget Durbar Square and the moment when Aunt could have turned around and changed history. Some days this was the only pure thought that I had left. But my future was set. Tsukri would be shunned by her own as an *adhiya*, a common free agent prostitute.

After several weeks, I passed my companion from our trip to Mumbai. Her eyes deep in their sockets, she whispered like the ghosts of Durbar Square. "Are we going to leave here dead or alive?" I did not know, and then another part of me believed that the decision had already been made, that death was only a transition and sometimes it arrived ahead of the body. Like the rest of us without a soul, my companion floated away and down the hall.

On my first day outside in two years, I saw the *adhiya* walking the dirty streets in bright red and hot pink saris. Their jewels looked as flimsy as their alluring smiles. Men called for their company with mere pocket change—a pitiful wage to match *adhiya*'s underappreciated work. Like beggars, the women clutched at the men as they passed. I wanted to shout out in their defense, so surprised that I would put anything I thought into words, but I was on my way to the doctor for my first abortion at a cost that was tallied upon my debt. Tens of thousands of rupees were still leveled against me, and years of work lay ahead. If I received a tip from a client, the money was stolen no matter where I hid it. In the evening after my doctor's visit, I was back at work, serving my debt. At least the *adhiya* had the freedom of the streets.

On a slow day, after two in the morning when the clients put their desires to rest—in a real bed like one I would never know—I listened to a man gasping just three curtains down from mine. He was with my companion, the ghost from the hallway. I knew her name, the name we shared—tsukri.

Tsukri's client made the promises that a man made when he pretended to love you. Some used the word "love." This type of client might beat you, and I usually saw it coming. When he was done, shame filled his eyes, echoing my own. I was a mirror of shame, a shadow of love, but with his fists, a man might erase his shame, pass it to me in double and make it all mine.

During my first two days in Mumbai, after being sealed alone in a room and made to watch pornography for hours, after being starved for the first of countless days to maintain my slender weight, I climbed from the window and dropped to the courtyard. A country girl understood that her new business was allowing men to do what they shouldn't, commit acts that not even the water buffalo or wild dogs would consider. However, my ankle was twisted from the fall, and as I limped toward the gate leading to the street, *gharwali*'s guards seized me. How foolish I was to attempt an escape. With no friend in the red light district or the whole of Mumbai, I was *gharwali*'s property.

For my flight, *Gharwali*'s cane crashed upon my hidden places without mercy, but I showed no tears. Building an image of the spire in my homeland, I transported my-self to the brilliant green mountains. For a few seconds, the scent of wild orchids reached me. I held my spirit above the filth and fake love of this hellish unnamed street.

The soles of my feet throbbed and swelled for hours. After convincing myself that the worst was over, five men entered my room, held me down, and gang raped me until I blacked out from the pain. They had set a price for my virginity, which they now understood would not be bartered easily, and so they made me pay instead. That was all that I remembered about my initiation, except for the defeat and the understanding that I was not strong enough to hold my soul aloft forever. In an instant, I'd lost hold of the silken threads that attached the spirit to the flesh. In the morning, I was told that this would happen every day until *tsukri* fulfilled her debt, paid back the money given to my heinous aunt, who sold me for cash to furnish her home in Kathmandu and tallied a karma debt that was taller and wider than Everest.

Mommy has nothing to say because I am alone on the top floor of Caesar's Palace. I need to get fresh air, but in the Las Vegas desert, there is no noticeable air. I try to get higher, closer to the sky.

Her words smolder in my ears. Worthlessness is heavier to carry than I imagined.

Gaining access to the roof, I am already happier. Heights never scare me, but Mommy cannot stand them. If and when she finds me, she will be too terrified to enter the roof. Her knees will buckle. If she hasn't already, she'll call security to help retrieve me.

No matter. I am only creating space and time in order to release a string of emotions that have been boiling inside me for years, decades, and centuries even. Why is it that people ask children to do things they will not do themselves? Who gives them the right? And where is the real profit in destroying the future? I have to believe that everyone wants to be happy and content. In Nepal, I learned at an early age that if you surrounded yourself with misery, then misery was your constant companion. Karma is not a destiny; it is a choice.

At the edge of the building, watching the sun paint cinnabar strokes upon the desert sands at dusk, I see how much I have always loved being high and the sensation of flight. The ladder raises me to the lip of the building. Kicking off my shoes, I walk above the whitewashed columns and sculpted images of gods and goddesses. The lights are just coming on the tower, setting the fountains and palm trees awash in golden light below. It's all so beautiful that I must remind myself that nothing is real.

With a step that is easier than many I took in the past, I depart from the building ledge. The pigeons of London scatter. Nepalese clouds pass overhead. Blue taffeta flaps around my ankles. All of my lives defy their gravity. I am flying.

I soar past the hotel. Rushing, stumbling to grasp at my flight, I see people I've known—Bapa, Master James, Mum, all my mothers—the same in a way, unable to sate the bottomless appetites of life on terra firma. I am flying.

Like bees in a honeycomb, I view people through the windows. They appear normal inside their cutouts, their problems neither too big nor too small, fitting their places and rituals undisturbed. Like jeweled beacons, televisions flicker the messages of the world. Men and women embrace and dance. Tumbling on the carpets, children feign all the good and bad of the Earth, preparing for their futures. People sing, and no one breaks their songs. Many do not notice my flight, maybe a few do as a passing notion, but they are busy reaping the honey of their lives, unworried about their destinies.

This time I get to choose, and I choose to fly. They will find me and try to piece me back together, all of my lives into one, but I will be soaring through the air, over the desert of a million lives and girls without names, past the greedy hands and hungry souls.

Nesting

Are you in love with her, this...?"

"Jasmine." Hank saw Darcy pause in the doorway. She had stopped crying. A lit cigarette poked from her fist. With her eyes occasionally darting down the hallway, she put the cigarette to her lips.

"Do you love her?" she asked.

"Not yet."

"So what's the attraction?"

"I don't know." He watched her rotate toward him. Smoke curled about their faces, connecting them by the thinnest of threads. He could yank her back with a single lie, but he refused to play any more games. "She's good for me."

"That's your excuse?"

"It's not an excuse."

"It's the worst I've ever heard. When you fall in love, I guess you'll know what to say."

A year later, Hank wondered if she'd jinxed him. He was in love with Jasmine, and he lied all of the time.

◆

Seated on a cardboard box by his apartment door, Hank waited for the moving van. He pictured Jasmine clearing space in her closets and shampooing the rugs. In her purse was a lengthy to-do list. It was scribbled on the back of a coupon for donuts. She behaved as if the entire planet depended on her last urgent scrap of paper. Hank imagined her tight script and his most important task at the top of her list: *Quit Smoking*. She had already struck out the words with a fat red marker.

When his cell phone vibrated, Hank plucked it off a shoebox full of compact discs. "Hi, Jas."

"Where are you?"

"I'm still waiting for the truck." He listened to Jasmine from across town. She owned a yellow ranch home with a modest yard. He loved that tiny patch of grass. Never having a piece of land to call his own, he changed jobs like dirty shirts, occupying a string of crummy apartments about town. Getting a permanent address represented another step up the ladder, although he wasn't exactly sure where it led.

"I just got back," Jasmine said.

"Everything go off all right?"

"I left him with my sister. He's out of the house."

"It's only a bird, you know."

"Yeah, I know."

"Parrots live a long time. It had other owners before you."

"I guess."

He clutched his fist in victory. He hated that bird, and the feeling was mutual. Whenever he laid a hand on

Jasmine, her parrot spouted phrases like a person with Tourette syndrome. Hank tried not to take it so hard, but after one particularly romantic evening when he kissed Jasmine goodnight, he swore the bird yelled "loser!" By the way Jasmine blushed, he knew it was something with that sentiment. *Who taught the bird to say that?*

"It will adjust." Hank refused to engender the bird. It was fitting that they were both relocating on the same day. The equation was simple: bird out, Hank in.

"When I get there, I'll make dinner." He planned to lift her spirits. Before Jasmine had inspired him to get a better job, he had worked as a short order cook. He could stretch the limits of whatever lingered in the refrigerator. "What are you in the mood for tonight?"

"The important question is," Jasmine asked, "how are you doing?"

Hank checked the nicotine patch beneath his sleeve, wondering if he'd correctly read the directions. Maybe it needed to be right on his throat, or at least his chest near his lungs. "The first week is supposed to be the hardest."

"It's been more than a week, hasn't it?"

"Ten days, I think."

"I'm so proud of you."

"Thanks." He placed his hand over the receiver and toked on a Marlboro. Unlike the one Jasmine stamped in the gutter last week, this was his final smoke. The image of a virgin cigarette being ruthlessly crushed still haunted him. At the time, he had considered scooping it up and smoking it anyway.

"You're taking it well," she said.

"For you... anything." He took another toke. There was no turning back. This time he would really quit. His lease was torn to shreds, and his stuff was jammed into a haphazard array of boxes and plastic bags. Tonight at Jasmine's, he would be going cold turkey.

"What's that sound?"

"What sound?"

"I keep losing you."

He turned his head, exhaling through his nose. "Nothing."

"You should get that phone checked. It's staticy."

"It's a company phone." Since last winter, he had been working in a roofing supply warehouse, his longest stint ever.

"Tell the company to replace it."

"I don't know."

"When you make manager, ask for a new phone."

There she was again, his private cheering section edging him toward success. "I shouldn't be using it for personal calls."

"They'll never know."

Hank glanced at the cigarette box, seeing a row of pure white filter tips staring back at him. He considered another farewell smoke, but, outside his window, he heard the hissing brakes of the moving van. "They're here. Gotta go."

"See you at home."

"What's that?"

"You know, *our* house."

It was her house, but he did not mind the casual association. By habit, he stashed the cigarettes in his jacket and slapped the nicotine patch for good luck. "See you there."

◆

With Hank's stuff piled in the center of Jasmine's living room, he was alone in the backyard, watching the sun retreat over the neighborhood. Like a lot of people, he used to poke fun of the suburbs, but spending time at Jasmine's place, he had reconsidered his opinion. For all of the chatter about tract housing and suburban blight, a backyard formed the unique signature of a contemporary homeowner—manicured gardens, aboveground swimming pools, toys and bikes scattered about the lawn. Jasmine had an understated style—a brick patio, wrought iron furniture, and stone urns with geraniums gnarled from over-pruning.

In the past, Hank had spent most of his time in her yard, grabbing a quick smoke, but standing there without a smoldering cigarette in his hand, he felt like a man who had recently lost a limb. He accepted the necessary suffering to reach his goal, and the only part he would change about his new domestic arrangement was the birds.

A flock of pigeons descended upon the lawn, preparing to foul the birdbath and then scratch the grass bare in spots. *Why did Jasmine put up with this?* She even spread birdseed on the lawn to encourage them.

As the flock milled closer, Hank searched his vest pocket for something to toss at them. He used to flick lit matches and cigarette butts, until Jasmine asked him to stop littering the yard. Maybe Jasmine's parrot had fostered his dread of birds, maybe not, but these pigeons made his skin crawl. They behaved like a wild band of scavengers—rats with wings.

One bird kept to the periphery of the flock, plodding nearer to Hank. It was slate-colored and had a crooked beak, and, as the sun flashed through the clouds, oyster shell speckles of color reflected upon its wings.

"Beat it!" Hank stamped his foot. If he had evicted a beloved parrot, he could persuade vagrant birds to roost elsewhere, but this pigeon waddled forward as if harboring no desire to live. Right then, he named the bird "Butch" after an old neighborhood kid with a deformed hand that had hung around the fringes of the other boys on the block. The Butch in Hank's memory had neither joined the regular crowd of boys nor fully escaped them. Hank hadn't seen the kid in years, but here was a pigeon with a twisted beak acting as Butch-like as ever.

Scooping a handful of change from his pocket, he tossed it at the flock, and the birds scattered. With its twisted beak clenched on a penny, Butch rose in the air.

"Don't spend it in the neighborhood." Hank watched the flock disappear above the roof. A few landed on the chimney, where bird droppings stained the asphalt tiles like bright white mud.

"Your days are numbered." He considered buying poison or at least some type of repellent. Across town, the hardware store sold owl decoys, and he wondered if they really scared the birds.

In the next yard, Hank spotted a woman leaning against the rusty metal retaining wall of a swimming pool. She was taking it all in, seemingly amused by Hank's pigeon rant. Glancing back at her house, she puffed on a cigarette. She seemed concerned with a vacant window on the second floor.

Hank recognized the telltale signs—the furtive tokes, the latent energy, the paranoia. She was ostracized from her own house, stealing a smoke. He felt her pain. At the very least, he too wanted a crisp cigarette in his mouth— the feel of the filter tip between his lips, the sheer pleasure of nicotine running through his veins.

In the kitchen, he found Jasmine standing beside the distressed wood table and chairs. The paneled walls were painted white, and small pictures of lighthouses hung from lace ribbons. Ice splintered in a glass of Chardonnay.

"What are you doing?" She wore blue jeans and a lavender shirt that picked up the violet specks in her eyes. Hank thought she'd busted him pitching coins at the pigeons, but instead she waived an opened pack of Marlboros in her hand.

"Where did those come from?" he said, as if never before laying eyes on cigarettes bound up in colorful cellophane-wrapped cartons.

"They fell out of your jacket."

"Mine?"

She clutched the faded denim in one hand, the offending cigarettes in the other. "They're not mine."

"How'd they get in there?"

"You don't know?"

Spotting his escape window, he leapt through it. "I thought you dumped my last smokes."

"Apparently not."

Good, she wants to believe me. The illusion of trust was critical. He might say anything to preserve it. "They must have been in there since last year."

"Didn't you wear this jacket on Tuesday?"

"I did?" Hank shuffled to the refrigerator to bury his head inside—either in there or in the oven with the gas cranked up. He couldn't play stupid forever.

After pretending to read a few labels, he shifted three or four jars on the door. He needed a smoke so bad that he wanted to rip that pack from her hand. Rubbing his nicotine patch, he prayed for a burst of soothing chemicals.

When he looked up, he saw her crushing yet another pack of cigarettes in the trash compactor. The machine vibrated, obliterating his emergency smokes. A half-dozen times last week, he'd witnessed this butchery. The trash compactor flattened and mauled his final smokes without conscience. Somewhere the Marlboro Man shook his head in disgust.

"You know," he said, "we don't have anything for dinner."

"What do you need?"

"This and that."

Turning away from the compactor, she removed the shopping list from the refrigerator magnet. "What are you making?"

He needed to get lost for a while. Much like the weeks spent waiting for his tax refund to arrive, he needed time and distance for his lies to become fact. "You don't want to ruin the surprise."

He kissed her and snatched his jacket from her hand.

She squinted, still holding the thread of her inquiry.

"I won't be long." He slipped out the door, before she caught her breath and posed another question.

◆

As Hank pushed a cart through the supermarket, a fat man in an orange jumpsuit mopped the cereal aisle. In the next aisle, a woman ordered a pound of spiced ham at the deli counter—"paper thin." Somewhere a toddler wailed without consolation. Trying to keep his feet moving in a forward direction, he let his skittish pulse navigate the store. In the past, he garnered disapproving stares as he dropped cartons of Marlboros into his cart. Today the world received him, ignorant of the nicotine copilot beneath his sleeve.

In the liquor section, he scanned the shelf for cooking wines. He decided to make Veal Napoleon to gain victory. He had impressed other women with the dish, and he believed that he'd already cooked it for Jasmine, but when he asked, she said no. The line between his old girlfriends and Jas was blurred. She had modified his life in one hundred ways. After convincing him to stay in the supply warehouse job, she had talked him into saving money and buying a car. Later on, she persuaded him to move in with her. "Two can live as cheaply as one," she said. Hank regularly ignored these advances from women, but while others skirted around their true intentions with vague promises of sex and meaningless favors, Jasmine landed her points with unmatched debating skills. He loved Jas, unable to resist her no-nonsense pressure. In a very real way, he believed that she was either going to make his life perfect or kill him.

A tinted glass door separated the liquor section from the bar next-door. When it swung open, the allure of burning cigarettes drew Hank inside.

At the padded bar rail, he nursed a cold beer. What was the harm? He needed a drink after his day of total commitment. Putting his head back, he inhaled the secondhand smoke from the old lady drinking old fashions. When she gave him a double take, he had to stop.

Across the room, he spotted a blonde. He admired her silky locks and the attractive shape of her shoulders beneath a flimsy ochre-colored tank top with spaghetti straps. As she turned back toward the counter, he waited for a glimpse of the face to match the body. His libido knew, moments before his brain. He'd been watching Darcy. What were the odds? She didn't even live in this neighborhood.

Darcy smoked Marlboro Lights in the gold pack. He recalled the weaker taste. Whenever he bummed a cigarette from her, he wound up smoking twice as many.

Right now, one poked from between her split fingers. He felt the safety of being among sympathetic souls. Never once had the phrase "I should really quit" left her mouth.

Sliding her gin and tonic from the counter, she walked around to meet him. She was a natural blonde with a permanent tan, and in the low light of the neon beer signs, the embrowned lines beneath her eyes took on a sandy appearance and her hair glowed like an advertisement of its own.

"I see you're still alive," she said. Dialogue for them had resembled a tennis match, all volley with no points to win or lose. The problem with a game like that was it never ended, unless you quit. He had quit on their volley. He saw that very clearly.

"You look good," he said, wondering if he should apologize for something.

"You look the same." She exhaled in his face.

He smelled the smoke, gin, and perfume—trace elements of their former relationship. Jasmine created a whole different chemistry—dried flowers, Chardonnay, and Lysol Scent II.

Darcy stabbed her cigarette pack toward him. "Want one?"

"No, thanks."

"Don't tell me you stopped?"

"I won't then."

"What happened to you?"

"I shouldn't smoke." He pictured Jasmine at home, scrubbing the sink, the tub, the slightest dirt from the toughest corners. He wasn't in a good place right now.

"I get it." She raised an eyebrow. It was a silent acknowledgment like he'd done with the woman behind Jasmine's house. It reminded him of the moment in his doorway when they'd split up for good. After saying good-bye, she'd crushed a cigarette butt in the hall like a calling card. With a quick flick of the fingertips, a smoker knew how to litter in a carefree and spiteful way.

"I've gotta go." He abandoned his beer and Darcy at the counter. He was afraid to look around to see if it mattered.

By the doorway leading to the street, the cigarette machine came alive with color as sunlight flooded the space. Packs lined up like soldiers at the ready. His pack—Marlboros with the red and white delta crest—held rank above the others. For a long time, Hank stood at attention.

◆

Parked behind the Seven-Eleven, Hank ripped into a fresh pack and lit up. Wonderful smoke fogged the cabin of his car. He was a New Jersey smoker. No restaurants, public places, or airplanes existed for him any longer, and so a smoker found a secluded niche, airtight and sealed off from the increasingly sterile world. A non-smoker did not understand how much a real smoker enjoyed these clandestine moments. It was a grand dismissal of every-thing green and all the people who existed to redirect your life like a communist reeducation camp.

He felt guilty, a primary emotion mixing with the tar and nicotine. It was all part of the experience. He took solace in surviving his encounter with Darcy, realizing that he still had time to sort out this smoking issue, lots of chances. As smoke fogged his view of the street, he touched his arm patch for good luck. Jasmine was a rock. After a couple more days with her, he might be cured.

While the cigarette in his hand drew closer to the filter, Hank thought of that kid Butch from the old neigh-borhood. Butch used to fumble with the baseball and scoop it up like a mitt in one hand, and the other boys mocked him. He never seemed to fit. Tough luck, Hank thought. Life was not fair, never level, and even though his part in old crimes was small, Hank could never make up for them, not truly.

Hank pushed his cigarette butt through the slit in the window and pulled out from behind the Seven-Eleven.

At the house, Hank saw pigeons on the front stoop. Picketing his return, they bobbed and strutted in circles by the door. Butch with the crooked beak led the march, scratching angrily at the turf. Hank plucked a fat mush-room cap from the bag and hurled it at the flock. It was the first thing that he had grabbed from the bag.

The pigeons dove on the mushroom, tearing it to shreds. Butch snatched a large chunk in his odd beak, shaking the beige veggie like a piece of rubber. The bird offered Hank that one-eyed bird stare, the one that said: Although I am smaller, I can rise above you and shit on your head.

Hank stomped toward the door.

Up and over the house, the bird disappeared.

He raised a fist and exclaimed for the world: "Ex-ter-mi-na-tor!"

◆

After locating Jasmine in the kitchen, Hank crept behind her to unload his groceries. She was leaning over the sink, shaving the skin from a cucumber. Cupping his hand over his mouth, he tested his breath one last time. He'd already chewed and swallowed four breath mints and spit out his gum through the car window, but when he kissed her ear, she flashed a panicked look.

He coolly removed the chardonnay bottle from the paper sleeve and rested it on the counter. "I stopped in the liquor store for wine."

She looked at him as if she knew everything he'd done wrong in the last decade and probably did, probably kept a list for that, too.

"You know how they smoke in there," he said.

"But the wine's in the dry goods half."

"I figured that out."

"Oh."

With out fully turning toward her, he gave the one-eyed bird stare. Why blow it now? Not for one lousy cigarette.

◆

As if the day had turned in his favor, the balance of the evening passed more smoothly than Hank had antici-pated. He won the night with his cooking, and later they cuddled in the living room with chilled glasses of wine. His possessions stood in three distinct piles on the floor. While he had been shopping, Jasmine had taken it upon herself to unpack his belongings and organize them by use and size.

She left to take a shower, preferring to shower twice per day. On weekends, Hank skipped showers, another habit he would have to modify.

As the pipes squealed and the shower gurgled down the drain, Hank monitored the noise from the spare bed-room. The window sash was raised, and a little electric fan spun and hummed, pushing the air at his back. Drawing from a Marlboro, he poked his head outside, shooting the smoke far past the windowsill. A handful of pigeons milled on the lawn, searching for an evening scrap.

Hank stared into the cigarette pack, assigning days of the week to each smoke in receding numbers. By next Saturday, he would be smoke-free, with Jasmine none the worse for wear.

When the water stopped, Hank pinched the remain-der of his cigarette between his thumb and forefinger and flicked it across the lawn. The glowing butt reminded him to clean up the lawn in the morning, but suddenly Butch snatched it up and flew off.

"Thanks, partner." Laughing, he popped a breath mint in his mouth. It was his turn to shower and cleanse away the sins of the day.

◆

Making love that night, Hank realized that by meeting Jasmine, he'd started an incredible streak of good luck. He'd been on his way to quitting the warehouse job, when he sat beside her on the bus. Preoccupied with words for his boss, he must have appeared cool and aloof and she mistook it for confidence. Right then, she probably decided a number of aspects about him that he might have to fulfill. He thought of them as goals to which he might aspire—his better self. What did her list for him look like? Pondering his own list of life improvements, he realized that Jasmine's list was likely more complete and written with better handwriting and spelling.

◆

While asleep, Hank dreamed that his willpower had grown tenfold. Standing in a room full of smokers, he had no desire to bum a cigarette. A plug had been pulled in his brain, and those awful urges drained away forever. He had completely licked the problem. Somewhere in the room, the kid Butch's hand worked almost like everyone else's and no one noticed his defect.

When the smoke detectors engaged at 3 am, Hank awoke to a high-pitched ringing in his ears. Jasmine was grabbing his arm and screaming. Smoke gathered on the ceiling like a map he couldn't read. For more time than he should have, he stared at the wispy patterns.

Jumping to the carpet, he moved on impulse, guiding Jasmine through the window. As he went, he swiped his keys and cell phone from the nightstand. The couple collapsed on the lawn, coughing. His eyes and throat burned, but he still had the sense to punch 911 into his cell phone.

Flames flickered on the roof near the chimney. Maybe a lightning strike or faulty wiring was the cause, but it seemed like an odd place for a fire to start.

The fire department worked for thirty minutes to get the situation under control. Running the hose from the corner hydrant, they sprayed the roof until water flowed over the front doormat and nothing inside remained dry. Near the end of their routine, a fireman propped a ladder against the front gutter and poked the charred beams with a metal rod, checking for embers.

With his arm around Jasmine, Hank sat on the curb, the taste of ash on his tongue. He wasn't going to smoke ever again. Breathing in chemicals from the burning house had overdosed him. Cigarettes were more than a bad habit. They were slowly polluting his soul.

The fire captain was short and husky, and his fire coat hung about him like a bed sheet wrapped around a

Christmas tree. "His wife says they haven't used the fireplace in weeks."

Hank favored the misconception and the idea that he and Jasmine could form a successful union. His swift reaction to the fire had empowered him, charging him the courage to face a bigger future. Without the slightest prompting from her, he was planning to find a better job.

However, Jasmine's house was destroyed, and she sobbed like a child, unable to create words from her spiked emotions. He held her like a crystal egg, like a perfect thing under his protection. There was real beauty in finally being the hero of his own life.

He adjusted the rescue blanket around her and gathered her head to his shoulder. "It's going to be all right."

Flashing lights and the moan of heavy equipment ruled the street. Pigeons collected on neighboring roofs, peering down on their old haunt. From the roof up, the house was wrecked, a charred and smoldering spine rising above the windows. Water ran over the sills and the front steps, cutting rivers and streams toward the curb.

Hank squeezed Jasmine. "We'll rebuild." He added another task to his mental list of life improvements: *Fix the House.*

A fireman stepped off the ladder and approached the captain. In his hands was a charred pile of twigs and straw. "Take a look at this."

"I'll be damned," the captain said, pushing his helmet up on his forehead. "A bird's nest."

"Right near the source," the fireman added, shaking his head. "Amazing it survived the blaze."

"There's no blueprint for fire."

One of the cops shined his flashlight on the spiky construction. "Don't tell me a bird was playing with matches?"

"Years back, I saw one collect smoldering matches."

"No kidding."

"But more than likely it was a lit cigar or cigarette."

Hank sensed Jasmine stir, and as her head lifted from his shoulder, she ceased whimpering. He felt the weight of her violet eyes upon him and flinched.

"Did you hear that?" she said.

He held onto her even tighter, trying not to look into her face.

"Hank?"

She awaited his next response, and, as time collapsed like the dying embers of the last cigarette in the pack, Hank knew he needed his best excuse yet.

The Trade

They met at a ten-day flea market in an abandoned train depot. Jewel spread her coveted collection of figurines across a linen tablecloth bequeathed by her mother. Kit wondered over Jewel's colorful little animals and children in poses. Jewel had named them all—a cheery collie called Star, a thrashing boy named Bert, a porcelain shoe dubbed Scuff—hundreds of them. Pretending to be each figurine, she carefully unwrapped them, whispering their secrets. Kit believed that Jewel didn't want to sell a single item, and as she lured passersby into conversation, he watched her entertain a few trades with no resolution.

Kit's table sat beside hers, overflowing with more junk from the past than seemed possible. Not yet sure of Kit, Jewel believed he'd stolen most of his booty and queried him with the scrutiny and urgency of a detective. She shook the tin bell that had hung from the neck of a circus cow, cranked the victrola that he bartered for a set of tires from the original Batmobile, and ran her fingers over the silverware that had once belonged to General Lee's daughter. These artifacts reeked of foreign danger, but mostly they had junked up his life.

At other flea markets, Jewel and Kit had crossed paths, eyeing each other's wares, listening to the incongruent statements people volleyed while chatting. Jewel told a Brazilian man that she might have been a dancer but her feet were made for hiking. As a jet roared overhead, Kit told a woman from Texas that he used to fly but lost his flying papers. He was suspicious that he'd mistakenly bartered them for a smoked glass mirror that dimly reflected the past.

The sun cut mysterious angles through the clouds, and the humidity formed an invisible veil that dulled the senses—all but Jewel's and Kit's, which stood acutely on edge, almost painful to the touch. Leaving his junk unattended, he asked to examine her collection of blue angels. She cautiously agreed, more scared of her attachment to them than his handling. Easy to miss, the angels were tiny, revealing more detail than first glance. They dotted the landscape of his palm, singing in a way he hadn't heard prior. For as long as she tolerated, he held them to the eerie light. His fascination was trade-worthy.

"What will you swap for these?" he asked.

Jewel experienced the kind of clutch in her heart one gets only a handful of times or less. "I don't know." The clutch itself was not the challenge. The blue angels had come into her possession after years of searching and heartbreak. Whether to let go, whether to keep safe was the question.

As she drifted through the junkyard of his lifetime, a pleasant fear consumed his soul. She picked up a crown from a forgotten king. With a deep wind, she blew hot breath across a map of the constellations. She massaged the rust from the tines of a trowel that had once reached for the moon.

"Why do you want the blue angels?" she asked.

Jewel recognized his expression. Kit was closing off, thinking about the next piece of junk to collect, but nothing was as desirable as those blue angels.

He took a step to pull away, but stopped short of committing that wholesale error and letting his past crush his future.

"Why do you want them?" she asked again.

"Because you didn't tell me," he said, "and I saw them anyway."

The Dog

Our dog was a German Short-haired Pointer named Greta, with vanilla-chocolate fur that smelled of decaying leaves when wet, which was as often as possible. A bird-dog never shies from water, cutting through the shallows of lakes and streams like an invading troop. Searching for water, Greta seized upon open spaces with jailbreak speed. In all seasons, we kept the front door sealed, making cautious passage, preparing our legs as blockers. I'd witnessed the dog's ears perk as the doorknob turned and the latch clicked free. No matter where she lay in the house, the dog leapt to the pads of her feet as if sniffing the daylight slicing through the crack. And Greta ran with enviable desire.

In proportion, the dog was smarter and more resolute than her keepers. She controlled our family, even as we leashed her to the pantry door. Learning to enter the back porch with a single paw, she pulled the screen door wide enough to pass, escaping into the yard as she pleased. If food slipped from our plates, she would snatch it midair, never letting it hit the floor. She was vigilant, always watching. Before the rest of us thought to hide, she heard my father pulling into the driveway and slid behind the couch. I recall this now, as my own children cling to me upon arrival. Greta knew that the back of the couch, beneath the coffee table, and the dark corridor in the center of the house offered refuge during sirens, lightning storms, and the aftermath of a bad day at the office. Greta was a savant of perception, a genius of reaction, skills I've honed over decades to mere workability.

On a Saturday in the fall when the air felt dry and braced the skin in the late afternoon, I rode my green bicycle with the sparkled banana seat and sissy bar. In those days, only professionals and old people owned bicycles with handbrakes. The rest of us either slowed gracefully to a halt or reversed the pedals and skidded. I was a third grader, skidding preferred. Racing toward the garage, turning, dropping one leg as I reversed with the other, I scraped the cement with black rubber, stopping just short of the painted white overhead door.

I tested the handle. Usually the garage door was locked from the inside, and it felt like an incredible weight, when in fact it would never budge. This time, the door lifted fast and light, springs creaking, rollers turning over rickety metal tracks—a glorious noise to an eight-year-old boy. The heavy door rose as if I'd thrown it into the air, as if I was stronger than my age.

Before I edged my tire over the uneven lip of cement that separated our home from the street, Greta rushed into daylight. I gripped my bike handlebars and watched her gallop toward the nearest intersection of our suburban neighborhood. Her paws reached and gathered, extended and crossed, as only an animal astride can do.

My father emerged from the shaded interior of the garage, near the tool bench piled with abandoned projects. Immediately I knew that he'd locked the dog inside for a purpose that I would never understand, other than to keep her penned in a single place at a certain time. This decision surprised me as much as my timely arrival for dinner had caught him off-guard.

He approached, hot and sweaty from a weekend project that a white-collar executive would rather avoid. "Stupid son of a bitch."

Of course, he wasn't referring to the dog. I'd already concluded that my father and I were different—my pensive ways, never saying what I felt, hesitant to a fault and failure. Insulting me didn't reflect badly on him, not even when he barbed me in front of the neighbors for laughs.

Expecting to be smacked, I waited for the burning sensation that followed a swipe across the head. To this day, I cannot hear well with my left ear, and I guard against being blindsided that much more. Boxers know that a right-hander strikes the left side. As for me, whether debating politics, religion, or the total on a dinner check, I spy for the punch. I prepare for the sudden repercussions of being wrong or at the wrong place at the wrong time. There is a hand that waits to rise and block.

Dad burned from his miscalculation. I'd complicated an imperfect day at home. Built for bars and boardrooms, he dominated places where adults assembled to pretend like kids without a mission. He understood false faces and tales, laughs on cue, and reassuring morbidity. I was the variable he couldn't avoid, the one who never respected the unstated rules. The one who wanted the truth.

Across the overflowing boxes and piles of trash, he gave his command. "Don't come back until you get her."

Shedding my bike in the doorway, I ran like Greta.

◆

The dog was champion of the tease and chase. I'd played it with her on occasion but never this late in the day, alone, or with my father so angry—not with this much at stake. Usually Mom gathered my three sisters and me into the sky blue station wagon, and we would tail the dog around the block, begging from rolled down windows for Greta to rejoin us. She always did after what seemed like hours but was no less time than it took for the pasta water to over-boil on the stove.

"That's it," Mom often threatened. "I'm doing something about this." She vowed worse and in specific detail—abandoning the dog, a one-way trip to the vet— but invariably the punishment was a few hours on the leash at the pantry door, where we visited our incarcerated family mascot in shifts, showering her with more attention than she'd gotten in weeks. The dog's perception of events amounted to this: free play through the neighborhood, including an investigation of neighboring garbage cans; a ride in the family car with her head out the window, ears flapping in the breeze; and temporary confinement for a nap and private petting sessions with the kids, culminating in a full dinner after dark. A good percentage of the human population would settle for this day-capping ritual.

By myself, Greta sensed my vulnerability, which I often wore upon my forehead in a furrowed brow. I was certain that everyone noticed and the dog recognized it, too. She passed the miniature windmill outside McGory's house where I'd planned my first attempt to take hold of her metal-studded collar. She pranced past the Martino's ever-growing curbside trash heap and the Steiner's perfect garden beds. Keeping at least twenty yards ahead, she measured my steps. Each time I stopped, the dog paused, glancing over her shoulder. If she didn't see me moving, I'd close the gap, but Greta knew.

At the corner, she eyed me longer than usual. I suppose she saw a chubby kid in a striped shirt with short sleeves and blue jeans with raggedy patches on the knees. She sniffed anxiety in the air, the scent I carried in most situations, the stench of stifled breaths on the sporting field, during tests at school, and in conversation with others. From a distance, Greta's eyes looked brown, but they were almond-colored and wild up close. Scrapping a paw in the patchy lawn beside the curb, she made an unpredictable move. She turned left instead of right. A right turn led us around the block, and in the past she had never circled more than twice, yet always circled. Today she turned left, leaving harbor for the first time.

I imagined my father's confession at home. Mom would notice me not washing my hands for dinner, the splash of water and soap that splattered mud across the bathroom counters. After checking for my filthy sneakers beside the door, she would search my sisters' faces and then my father's. She would recall the garage door rising, and then my father would have to speak. He would set the radio to a jazzy tune and rock my mother from behind, creating that invisible envelope where no other noise filled the house. With a whisper or a vague notion, he would make it appear as if he had warned me, as if I had volunteered to go, assuring her of my eminent return. The belief was that I had set events in motion, which I unknowingly had, but I swear from a distance of years that the day belonged to Greta. All decisions were hers.

The dog broke from the neighborhood, and as we traveled out of bounds, awe and loathing filled my heart. Greta was more interested in distance than learning, passing sights that had lit her imagination prior—a stack of car tires, piles of leaves, a split open bag of trash.

As we moved into unfamiliar neighborhoods, the houses stood stone-faced and quiet in the approaching dusk. In the late 1960s, Saturday night dinners had not yet been abandoned in the suburbs, and although a preponderance of drugs, rock'n'roll, and war would soon lay waste to tradition, tonight nuclear-decaying families gathered around tables, beyond the view of a boy and dog traipsing across driveways and unfenced backyards in neighborhoods where neither Greta nor I recognized the smells and sights or even the names of the streets.

I was lost without Greta, and she paused to let me catch up. With a whine that trembled in her throat, she called me, led the way. The few times in the past that she'd escaped unnoticed from the house, we couldn't find her for hours. Did this sleek running machine know where she was headed? Had she a secret path unknown to us?

◆

Near dusk, we reached Route 33 buzzing with traffic. Like the border between countries, the two-lane highway divided our town. The people who lived on the other side, we only met in school and church where the rules were formal and scripted to a common protocol. The highway was widely considered a "no cross zone," the only passport being an adult chaperon.

With traffic speeding from both directions, Greta waited beside the road. Would I catch her in time? Or would I witness her death as she leapt into a line of speeding cars? As she stepped onto the blacktop, I knew I had to follow her and accept a similar fate—anything rather than return home empty-handed or, even worse, with a dead or wounded dog that I couldn't possibly carry. At eight years old, I hadn't learned to cut loose the wild horses inside me that would one day almost destroy me, yet pull me back from the brink of a life wasted in anger and regret. By the roadside, I froze as the first car honked and the brakes engaged. The smell of burning rubber snapped me from a trance.

An army caravan was coming up from behind. A line of vehicles—canvas-roofed tractors, camouflage-colored jeeps, gun-wielding flatbeds, wagons, and supply trucks—stretched for miles out of sight. Greta stood before the lead truck, wagging her tail, barking at the driver. It was a canine conversation that no one translated, except that on her day of crossing borders and boundaries, she had stopped the U.S. Army dead in its tracks.

"Greta?" I eased after her. Car exhaust and motor oil filled my nose. The adrenaline rush of idling engines just waiting to run me down caused me to stagger. Stumbling toward the dog, I reached, grasping only the wind of her escape. She sprinted into the fields beyond the highway. I'd been so close, and I was finally angry.

"Damn it!" I shouted the curse words that were forbidden at home, school, and even in private. Stomping in pursuit of Greta, I heard her panting through the crunch of the dried weeds that rose to my waist. Stickers caught in my clothes and scraped my bare arms, and my sneakers sunk in the spongy soil until they were soaked and muddy. Part of me wanted the dog to race back into traffic and end the stalemate.

Instead, Greta brought me out into an unfamiliar neighborhood. Smaller houses than my own, their yards were cramped with rusted patio furniture and ramshackle sheds—décor as afterthought. A mile or more away, the spire to our church—just the tip of it—poked above the rooftops, and as dusk overtook daylight, a vengeful sun retreated into suburbs, setting the clouds on fire.

I'd been on the hunt for hours, sweaty and cold from the chase. My legs felt heavy, and blisters formed in unfamiliar places on my feet. Dropping to the curb, I was spent of breath and the little confidence that I'd mustered from the start. I'd been cheated from my moment of spite. When I left the house with my father's marching orders, I had intended to not return until I held Greta's collar. My father would have gotten her. He would've accomplished it. A failure again, I would have to face him, and I hated it. I hated everything, including my father. Tonight, I hated him as much as he hated me, almost as much as I hated myself.

Clearly I was nothing like the man who wanted little to do with his embarrassment of a son. This was the man who, on the day I was born, went to a bar and got drunk, rambled in celebration through the neighborhood, and handed out cigars. That was before he had gotten a good look at me. How could I have inherited nothing of the successful businessman, that skilled negotiator of deals and promises? My hands were slender, woman's hands, doomed to pencils and paper, quiet detail work, the scribe of complex thoughts and poignant undeclared statements, not the powerful grip of a man who handed out fistfuls of handshakes over cocktails and contracts. Too often I reminded him of his hidden, lesser self, while demonstrating none of his talents—a failed legacy. My father excelled in a crowd, best at acquaintances. People were his business, his clay to mold. I was unworkable, to be overlooked, a throwaway appointment on his calendar. Suffering in crowds, in threesomes even, my passion burned in other ways, better in one-on-one meetings, unearthing the details, best alone with women, not the son of a wife-beater who triumphed in humiliation as well, yet I made women comfortable with their words, thoughts, and nakedness expressed.

Greta sat on the grass several feet from where I hunched over my knees. I was full of sorrow and self-loathing, yet brimming with the anger that I would need to survive the future. I was alien, relieved to be in a place where no one knew my name. As a young man in my twenties, stranger would be my name, and my history would reveal a series of forwarding addresses.

As soon as I took to my feet, Greta ran off. The dog matched my slower pace. Trotting, stopping, allowing me to stay at her heels, she taught me to dance, moving deeper into the unfamiliar neighborhood. The fuse of my anger fizzled with the sunset. Exhausted, my emotion drained away, and a dividing line was drawn in the absence of fear. It was OK to hate my father, choose to despise him of my own freewill. I could bury it deep, make it the coal of the engine that drove me for the next decade.

◆

Beneath a carport to a tiny brown bungalow, a woman leaned from the doorway. Her hair was set in curlers and a hairnet, and in the glow of a yellow porch light and circling insects, she watched the cat and mouse game between Greta and me.

"Hey, kid," she called.

I knew to ignore strangers, but at the moment I had nowhere else.

"Hey, kid, does your dog like baloney?"

Greta loved any variety of table food. She even ate lettuce. She might throw it up later, but with a little salad dressing, she ate it.

"Sure," I said.

The woman disappeared into the carport door and returned with a cool slice of baloney. It was the cheaper kind that my mother bought when the better lunchmeat wasn't on sale. My stomach growling, I considered eating it myself. "Thanks."

As soon as I held the baloney in the air, Greta was at my waist. I snatched her collar like a person latching onto a railing or tree limb to avoid a greater fall.

"Ma'am, thank you." I held up the slice to return it.

"Give it to her, kid."

Greta gobbled down the baloney, licking my finger-tips. She never made a move to escape.

"Thank you," I said once or twice more. "Do you know where the highway is, ma'am?"

"Do you live around here?"

At that point, I told the first important lie that I can recall. I wasn't about to give up my liberation, escorted home in the rear seat of a stranger's car. "I'm around the corner. I've gotten confused, that's all."

She eyed me suspiciously. Kids and politicians are bad liars, although kids fess up a lot faster. "Just follow Wisteria to Adams and straight from there."

When I looked up at the purple sky, I remembered to follow the direction of the setting sun. At my back, blackness and a hint of stars absorbed the horizon. How hard could it be to find the highway with the compass of the sky? I already heard the cars and trucks roar over the rooftops—the same sound I heard from bed at night. I walked toward what I knew.

◆

In the thickening night, we traipsed through the streets. My back ached from bending over to grip Greta's collar, and I tripped on the uneven sidewalk so many times that my jeans tore, my knees bled into the frayed material, and my palms were as raw as scuffed leather, but I didn't care. I'd caught the dog and was returning home with her in tow. Once I walked through the front door, I would release her, and instead of cowering, I would face my father, mirroring his contempt. He could smack me until my ears rang into deafness, and I would stand there and take it.

With a glimpse of Route 33 and the neon lights of a familiar convenience store between the houses, I saw my long but certain path home. Greta tugged at her collar, and I dragged her to a standstill.

"Come on, girl." I yanked harder.

Whining, tugging backward, she resisted forward progress. Beyond the sidewalk lay a small park with an even smaller pond. In a day of firsts and newfound liberty, a day when I glimpsed my future self, I received a seminal moment of intuition. I released the dog's collar, and she headed straight for the water.

In the light of an early moon, I found a park bench to rest. The dog splashed and jumped, not unlike my kids do nightly in the tub—the joy of water, life, free of inhibition. That summer, Americans walked on the moon for the first time, while others lost count of the body bags coming home from overseas. No one paid much mind to me.

Bigger sensations were afoot than a dumb kid and a water happy dog in the park after hours.

For half an hour, Greta drenched herself in the cool autumn and then returned to my side. Shaking the dampness from her fur, she baptized me on the spot. This time she let me take her collar without resistance.

As we headed home, I didn't feel any different, but Greta had taught me how to be unbreakable—even when broken—and how to stick to my point despite my fears. Although it took years before I seized upon her advice and learned to ply it as my own, today I listen for the phantom creak of a door hinge, feel a slight draft in my soul, see the break of daylight as if it were my final chance—and then I set to running.

The dog's spirit was so strong that eventually my father put her to sleep and in a way defeated himself. Dragged before the needle on a cold stainless steel table of a vet whose name I cannot recall, Greta panted her last breaths with no one from the family allowed to ease her into the next phase. Certain images can never be fully imagined or forgotten, but I will always remember Greta. That late afternoon in October, I hold close, as if grafted to my heart.

Coffins

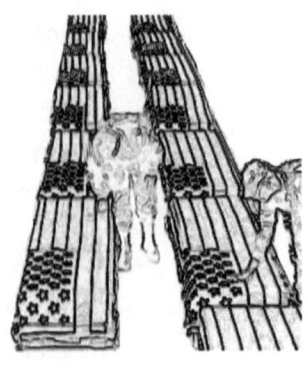

The idea was that Leo Harris got stuffed inside a laundry sack and let the seniors kick and punch him until exhaustion, tears, or whatever it was that made the seniors feel good. In September, Leo saw a freshman screaming with heat balm in his underpants. Like a crazy jackrabbit, the kid danced about the locker room floor to a chorus of cheers and awe. Other boys got their faces dunked in toilets, and they emerged from the stalls, hair dripping wet, pride shot to hell. Commode christenings, as they called them, were a big deal. After all, this was Holy Cross High School.

The plan for Leo's humiliation belonged to three varsity members of the football team. During fifth period on Tuesdays, freshman shared the locker room with upperclassmen. Their bigger more advanced bodies stalked the gym, sergeants in the boy hierarchy. At random, one freshman would be singled out, but everyone got his turn. It was easy to spot the uninitiated classmen of 1994. They were the only boys in the locker room still scared.

Except for Leo. He hated the seniors, and he shook only because he was angry. If they picked on him, he'd decided to knee one in the groin or bite one in a way that left a scar. Leaving a mark was worse than pain.

In bed at night, Leo allowed his revenge to blossom. He imagined years down the road, when the ogres of Holy Cross amounted to less. From a plush office, he would plot their misery without conscience, like a CEO who signed an order and one thousand people lost their jobs before lunch. That was really winning. Leo knew a thing or two about gaining leverage over your peers. During the summer, he'd read a biography on Bill Gates. You needed discipline and a plan. For a very long time, Gates carried a plan that no one noticed.

As steam wafted from the showers, the locker room smelled like sweat and half-hearted attempts with deodorant sticks. Locker doors slammed closed. Zippers tore across gym bags, and conversations buzzed about girls and homework—the shifting goals that tormented the lives of high school boys.

Avoiding the seniors' wrath in the early weeks, Leo had raced through the showers. He toweled off in a jiffy, and as he slipped into his underpants, he was still partially wet.

"In the sack." Jimmy Whalen lumbered closer. He had thick arms and rounded shoulders, perfect for a future vocation where his brain was not his primary tool.

Leo avoided eye contact. Maybe it wasn't him that they wanted.

Two seniors flanked Whalen. He stretched a laundry bag that had been snatched from the team room. The cotton hem snapped open. "In the sack, fishy."

Leo felt like cursing but swallowed his words. He glanced at the double swinging doors to the basketball court. Their gym teacher, Mr. Pappinger, was nowhere in sight, probably ogling the girls playing volleyball.

"Here... fishy, fishy."

Hardened from the practice fields, the approaching boys looked like bruised meat. Leo's thinner, tender body might fit inside any one of theirs. One day, he expected to exceed their height. His father was 6'1" and fast on his feet, but these aspirations didn't help Leo now.

"Heeeeere... fishy."

Leo dropped his shirt on the wooden bench. His pants hung in the locker along with his tie. There was not enough time to get dressed. As if he'd become contagious, the other freshman withdrew from Leo's vicinity.

"Into the sack," Whalen ordered.

"Can't we do this another way?" Leo immediately regretted saying this. A commode christening awaited those who resisted, or maybe it awaited him in any event.

"In!"

"Come on."

The boys started chanting, all but his closest friends joining along. "In! In! In! ... "

Leo broke for the space between the second and third boy, but these were football players, trained to close a gap faster than a police line. When he saw them shouldering together, he hauled up.

Whalen leaned forward, his fat front teeth just inches from Leo's eyes. "Nice try, fishy."

As the sack went over his head, he twisted and kicked until his bare feet left the slimy tiles and he flipped over with the laundry bag. For a time, he felt weightless, before his head clunked the wooden bench and then the floor. The elastic band of his underpants was ripped from his hips and along his thighs, fingernails gouging his skin. The boys knotted it shut and closed the bag in darkness.

Naked, breathing in the stench of past football drills, Leo writhed inside this locker room embryo. He cursed the seniors, individually and apart. He threw punches, but never challenged the stitches that bound the rough denim bag, only bashed his fist on the wooden bench. When he heard them mocking his futile attempts to get free, he stopped moving altogether and gasped for air.

"Fishy – fishy," Whalen taunted.

Their feet circled and slid around him, but not enough light seeped through the denim to offer clear shapes. Leo guessed their next move. A roll through the showers? A dunk in the toilet? This might be their joke. They would leave him for Mr. Pappenger to discover—alone, naked, and late for English class. News of his shame would light the ears of half the school.

After a short pause of whispers and laughs, they started punching and kicking him, whipping their belts into his legs, ribs, and arms. He curled into a ball, protecting his head with his forearms. Wincing, tears in his eyes, he never screamed, only registering the sound of his grunts below the boys cheering. His so-called friends had joined the chanting, friends who thought that Leo needed sight to witness their betrayal. He considered dying on the spot, just to spite the world.

But just as the beating verged on worse, it suddenly stopped. Leo heard a scuffle, followed by the sound of a body crashing into hollow metal. He swore it was Whalen who'd hit the lockers.

"I asked you guys to cut this out," someone said.

Leo was pulled up to a seated position, and a single pair of hands began undoing the knot.

"You all right in there?" The voice was deep but still a boy talking.

When the bag opened, Leo readjusted to daylight—a crash of white and clean air.

A big sophomore named Daniel McGinty offered a hand up. He had black curly hair and a broad reassuring smile. A kid who was physically years ahead of most, he was the star of the football team, but Leo didn't speak. Why was one of them helping him?

"They're not going to bother you no more," Dan said.

Leo spied Whalen and his buddies backing off. Filing around a row of lockers, they mumbled and cursed beneath their breath.

"There you go." Dan helped Leo to his feet. Naked, dripping wet, Dan must have walked from the showers to break up the hazing. His breast cut away in a smooth v-shape, and his abdomen scrolled around his waist. He looked flawless—the kind of body that they promised on television commercials and you never achieved. The mere sight of him in the nude quieted everyone.

"These guys get carried away," Dan said. "You know what I mean?"

"Yes." Even though his arms and legs were stinging, Leo was safe. He was years away from the understanding that pain and gracelessness affirmed his life.

Without another word, Dan went after his towel. The showers were shutting down one by one, and the mist clouded the tiled entrance.

Leo wanted to say thanks, but it was too late. Dan had moved onto another front. That was Daniel McGinty. He never lingered—no explanations needed, no grudges carried, and no thanks required. As if created in a perfect fusion of basic elements, Dan's awesome shape disappeared into the heat and steam of the showers.

Leo watched him go, and briefly, because one tended to record thoughts quickly and process them later, he realized that a man could be beautiful, too.

◆

As his father's car turned the corner, Daniel McGinty saw a giant donut eclipse the steeple of St. John's Church. The roof of Burrough's Bakery supported a huge fiberglass baker lifting an even bigger chocolate donut with multi-colored sprinkles over his head. Featured in three PBS specials over the years, the Hamilton landmark was rumored to be the inspiration for a line of Andy Warhol silk-screens. It created the kind of eyesore that you only noticed after living away from town.

"Stop the car," Dan said.

Dan was home from his first year at Penn State, and his toes were throbbing along the edge of his leg cast. The last thing he needed was a donut and milkshake. He felt flabby and weak from a winter of rehabilitation, and in the spring, a second operation to repair his torn knee ligaments further slowed his progress, but as soon as he glimpsed that giant donut, he knew what he needed to do. Things were looking up.

"Stop the car," Dan repeated.

After checking the rearview mirror, Dan's father hit the brakes on his brand new '94 Caprice. He still had the new car sticker in the window. "Mom's made your favorite dinner."

"I know."

"You aren't going to walk home?"

Dan sensed his father's protective nature, his inability to release him wholly into the world. This was what he loved about him. "You know me. I'll get a ride."

"Why are we stopping here?"

Peering inside Burrough's, Dan spotted the girls at the counter. "I need to talk to Heather."

"I thought you two broke up."

"It's complicated." Dan had never officially broken up with Heather, or was it the other way around? When Dan had left for college on a football scholarship, he'd warned her about long practices and difficult studies. He read to her quotes from Coach Paterno's orientation letter. He wouldn't have a minute to himself. Thinking he was only being fair to her, he was surprised when she cried. Each phone conversation became awkward and strained, and by Thanksgiving, they had stopped talking.

Dan slid his leg onto the sidewalk, leaving his crutches in the car. He wasn't a backward-looking guy, but their last conversation stuck in his mind. It had marked a pretty strange week. *The Sporting News* had dubbed him a young tight end to watch, and by the weekend, an unknown cornerback from Rutgers University had taken out his knee. At some point between Monday and Saturday, Heather had phoned for the last time. Not even after his injury did she phone him.

Through the open car window, Dan's father called to his son. "Don't be long."

"I won't," Dan said, but expected to be late. That meant he needed apologies for two women—Heather and Mom. He sure wished he'd spoken to Leo before doing this. Leo had an answer for everything, the only kid in high school with a day planner. This annoyed some people, but if Dan ever needed a long-range plan, Leo could map one out in minutes. No wonder Leo aimed for law school. He was halfway there already.

When the football star hobbled through the front door, the smell of chocolate and pastry hit his senses—a romantic vision of his childhood. Burrough's was famous for refried donuts to order, and as three people stood in line for donuts and spiced coffee, hot grease bubbled behind the counter.

Dan spotted Heather sugaring a cruller beneath the warming lights. Her auburn hair was tucked behind her ear, and she wrinkled her nose in a rarified way. This tick of hers was tangled up with his longing to find home again.

"Got one of those for me?" he asked.

Heather put down the sugaring tin. Her face aglow in the orange warming lights, she stared blankly at him.

"Don't say you forgot about me." He leaned against the counter.

"What do you want?" she asked.

"I'm not here for a donut, if that's what you think."

"What are you here for?" She touched the collar of her uniform dress. Her eyes seemed as white as the bleached cotton material.

"I came to see you." He figured that she would be angry. For sure, he'd blown it between them. Their time apart had taught him that much. "Can we talk?"

Heather grabbed the attention of the other girl who was busy wrestling with the latte machine. "Kathy, can you cover the counter for a few minutes?"

The people in line were annoyed at the suggestion of losing the only other counter girl, but Kathy took one look at Dan and agreed.

When they entered the alley between Burrough's and St. John's Church, Heather took a position against the cinderblock wall. Dan came closer, almost hovering. As the bells chimed, they both glanced up toward the spire and its corroded green cross.

Dan's toes pulsed against the blacktop. Without his crutch, he needed to brace one arm against the wall. It seemed like a long time since he had carried his weight as he should. "Hey, you like my cast?"

"Leo told me about it." She shrugged.

"You're mad at me, aren't you."

"That was months ago."

He almost asked why she still wasn't. "I guess I made a mistake."

"I can't believe this, Danny." She glanced at her watch, impatient. "You're doing this now?"

"Why can't you believe me?"

For the first time since he showed up at the bakery, he noticed her looking directly at him, really taking him in her sights. This pleased him until he couldn't read her expression. What was it with women, the way they veiled their innermost desires?

"Things changed when you left," she said. "You promised that would happen."

"I was just talking."

"It's not talk anymore."

"Hey, I'm sorry."

"I've got to get back. Kathy's alone at the counter." Pushing off the wall, she twisted her neck toward the bakery's rear door, and a silver chain slipped from the opening of her uniform.

Dan's eyes fell to the Holy Cross High School ring dangling from the links. For more than three years, his ring had hung from her neck, but that particular ring sat on the bottom of his junk drawer at home. When he had returned for winter break, it waited for him in a plain brown envelope—no note from her, just a simple return address. He wanted to check to see if it was still there.

Heather tucked the chain back into her uniform and pressed her hand against her chest.

"Whose ring is that?" Dan was already sizing up the man whom he needed to put away. He didn't require two good legs for that.

"We were going to tell you eventually," she said.

"What do you mean *we?*"
"Don't do this here. I'll call you…"
"Tell me," he said. "Whose is it?"
"It's Leo's," she said. "He gave it to me."

The 2001 law school graduation committee created an archway of blue and white balloons to be released upon the moment of degree. Leo Harris glanced down at the short hem of his black gown. He had grown into his size, not as wide as Dan but just as tall. When they had played baseball at Holy Cross, Leo stationed first base, and Dan covered second. Dan's movements were graceful and efficient, and to cover Leo's lack of depth, Dan regularly slid across the field and into Leo's space. He would stuff the ball into Leo's glove, saying, "We got it covered, old man."

Marching in for commencement, Leo saw Heather first. She worked as a nurse in Hamilton, a bright and beautiful young woman. He felt lucky to love her. It was the kind of impromptu thought that he needed to impart immediately and failed to mention later. With a glance, he hoped his eyes said everything.

Dan stood beside Leo's mother. When Leo's father had died suddenly of a heart attack, Leo was in his second year at college. Feeling unable to carry on with classes, he nearly applied for an incomplete grade and took a leave of absence, but Dan stepped in and was generous about checking on Leo's mom. Regardless of the fact that Dan and he had never discussed the business with Heather—a situation that might crush most friendships, one that in reverse Leo knew he wouldn't handle as well—Dan covered the bases at home.

It amazed Leo that Heather or anyone else remained blind to one simple fact: Side by side, Leo felt that he could never fill Dan's shoes. To avoid the obvious comparison, he had pushed himself far afield in academics.

The ceremony was long and overbearing. A senator, who was on his way out of office, gave a speech that reminded people why they weren't voting for him in the fall. Leo glanced back but didn't see Heather, Dan, or anyone he recognized.

At the conclusion, Dan came up on Leo from behind. Leo turned to take in the fullness of his face. He'd added a few pounds but didn't appear any less fit.

"Congratulations," Dan said. "Your mom gave me the news. Congratulations twice."

"Thanks." Leo had only proposed to Heather last evening. He'd wanted to tell Dan personally. Was it appropriate to apologize here and now for an unacknowledged past transgression? Did it matter this many years down the line? "I never really…"

"Hey, it's a good thing, old man. You make a nice couple." Dan shifted his weight, so slightly that only Leo noticed. His knee had never healed perfectly, making the remainder of his college football career less than stellar. Lacking the speed and quick cuts that made him distinct, he became an also-ran, and the pros skipped him in the draft. No team even invited him to camp for a tryout.

"I want you to be my best man," Leo said. "Is that good?"

"Sure is." Dan gave Leo a bear hug, lifting him off the ground.

Leo regretted not being able to offer Dan more. For so many years, he'd followed Dan's lead, wanting to be more like him than any person he knew. He longed to be beautiful and charitable, not stuck inside himself, having to work so hard to be real, but it appeared that Dan was stuck—caught in a dead end desk job with the state, grounded by fate and rotten luck in the form of a bum knee that wouldn't hinder a million other successes. It wasn't fair. Just as Leo stood on the precipice of his dreams, Dan was sinking into anonymity. This wasn't how the gods had designed Dan. Built for cheering crowds and adoring fans, he was supposed to be holding a trophy over his head. He was supposed to win.

By the fall of 2002, the public clamored for the heads of men in public office, and the very act of sweeping in a new administration pacified voters, because nothing ever changed in government except for the people. Daniel McGinty had heard that this meant less people in state jobs. Twice, Leo had phoned to warn him. A new governor was being sworn in on New Year's Day, preparing to wield a quick ax. In general, requital hung in the air, and talk of war befuddled the news pundits across the nation. In Washington D.C., the President pressed his sword to the grindstone and readied for battle abroad.

On Christmas Eve, Dan entered the offices of Blake, Cauthen, and Maglione. Fresh cut holly branches and tasteful miniature white lights decorated the front desk.

While typing into a computer, the receptionist handled clients over the phone like an air traffic controller, but she paused and gave Dan her full attention. "Thank God, you're here. The copy machine is in the back."

Dan was dressed in a flannel shirt and jeans. Was a sport coat and tie the right choice for a casual visit? "I'm looking for Leo."

"Mr. Harris? Do you have an appointment?"

"He's a friend."

"Excuse me, take a seat please." She pressed some buttons, and minutes later Leo was guiding Dan through the complex.

"Nice digs here." Dan glimpsed the offices as they walked the main corridor. Two men in three-piece suits exchanged gifts wrapped in flashy metallic paper and bows. A woman in a Santa cap snuck whiskey into her coffee mug. As Dan passed, many women glanced to check him over. Until Leo pointed it out last summer on the beach, Dan hadn't noticed this as much. Women always took in Dan's figure. He thought they looked at every man, which apparently wasn't true.

"Do you need a date for New Year's?" Leo asked in a low voice. "The office is loaded with possibilities."

"What would Heather say about that?"

"She knows I'm married to my job." Leo looked toward the stacks of paper on his desk. "Bankruptcy is an ongoing affair."

"That explains your long engagement. I'm still waiting for my wedding invitation."

"Some engagements last forever."

"Not this one, I hope."

Leo leaned back on the front edge of his desk. "What brings you here?"

Dan wanted to ease into the discussion, but inside Leo's office with his files of official paperwork and all the hard-edged wood paneling and squared-off furniture, the room seemed better suited for a debate than idle chatter. Not a single person, Dan thought, entered this place without a problem to solve. "I've got an idea."

"What kind?"

"A business prospect."

"For me?"

"Sort of. Well, yes." Dan took a seat on the couch. Walking or even running rarely bothered him, but the pressure of standing in one place aggravated his knee. He carried several quirky pains as reminders of his former life as a star of the playing fields, however, to reacquire that status, he would gladly take on several more. If only he could reclaim that state of being, always knowing he had a fighting chance.

"Let's hear it," Leo said.

"You keep telling me about layoffs coming my way."

"I didn't say it would be you. I was only warning you about the new political landscape."

"But I'm expendable, like you said."

"I didn't say that either. Maglione is well connected. He expects cuts in government payroll, especially the motor vehicles department. It's politics. That's all."

"I get that part, so I'm forming a contingency plan like you suggested."

"Tell me about it."

"I'm thinking of an on-line athletic equipment store."

"Do you have a business plan?"

"I've scribbled some things down."

"Did you research it? There are already places on the web."

"Well how about I open a gym?"

"Which is it, an Internet company or a gym?"

"Maybe a little of both."

Leo seemed to study him like a foreign map, like a play that Coach Paterno scribbled on the board which no one understood at first. "Where's the gym going to be?"

"Somewhere in town maybe, off the interstate or near the mall."

"Off the top of my head, there are three gyms around town. That's your competition."

"Maybe I should go back to my Internet idea." An on-line business suited his desire to stay clear of an office. "I was talking with my father. I could warehouse items at his place for a start."

"You need more than that." Leo readdressed the paperwork on his desk. "Do you know how many bankruptcies I handled this year? And these people had a plan, not a very good one, but they had a plan. A bankruptcy would set you back for years."

"I'm not planning on going bankrupt."

"These people didn't think so either."

Dan couldn't shield the fact that he had no firm ideas, other than waiting for Leo to tell him what to do next. If he had his choice, he would open a combined health food café and gym, like one he'd seen in New York, but he wasn't going to mention a complicated notion like that.

"I like your gym idea," Leo said. "You might be able to pull it off. You'll have to be the star of it, put yourself as an athlete on the masthead."

"You want me to perform."

"No, I want you to be the place, the face of the business." Leo ran his hand over the desk blotter. "How about buying a franchise?"

"This is all just talking out loud, dumb thoughts. I need to find another job, I suppose."

"Can I ask you a question?"

"Shoot."

"What do you really want to do?"

"I told you already."

"No, where do you see yourself in the future?"

Dan protected the truth, clutched it tight to his ribs like a slick football on a day when the game was challenging and the final score was not yet decided. It wasn't that he didn't know where he was headed. He knew, but with an unshakeable grip, his dreams held him in position. He never used to consider himself stuck. For years, he imagined walking onto a professional practice field during tryouts—the smell of the low cut grass and men waiting in anticipation of his next move. Magic happened every season. Walk-ons made the team, came from nowhere and stole a spot from an aging veteran or a young pretender on the bubble. But at twenty-seven years of age, he was the worse kind of pretender. His most sacred dream was never going to be realized. Deep down, he understood this as well as anything, as clearly as Leo was standing across the room. If Dan released these dreams, his future stood wide open in a way that disturbed him. It had to assume a form he hadn't yet conceived.

Gazing down the hash marks of his life, the gap between his reality and the past was yawning. He took to his feet again, preparing to tear up his dreams in front of his oldest friend and view the scattered pieces. This, he saw, was why he came here today.

"I want to play ball for the Giants," Dan said.

Leo let Dan's response sit between them like a pop up fly ball that had mysteriously parted two infielders and landed in the infield dirt. In disbelief, the players stared down at the gaff.

"Which one," he said, "baseball or football?"

"Either one would be fine." Dan studied Leo's expression. There was a weird twist to Leo's mouth.

"I thought you'd say that," Leo said.

"Yeah, I know. That's me."

"I know," Leo said. "I know."

◆

When Heather suddenly moved out, Leo took a leave of absence from the BCM law offices. This was ironic, because all that Heather had asked for was more time with Leo away from the office. As soon as she left, he sent her flowers, chocolates, and awful, heartfelt poetry that he scribbled in the dark. Heather sighed and crinkled her nose. He imagined the nose part over the phone, but mostly he moped about their gutted apartment like an abandoned puppy. All that was left behind was the garage sale furniture and the curbside salvage and that she had let him keep in the first place.

More than a week into this debacle, Dan arrived with camping gear stuffed into the bed of his pick-up truck. Hearing Dan's sputtering truck pull up outside, Leo rose from a ratty orange recliner and stuck his head out the window. In the background, the TV droned about efforts going both worse and better than expected in Iraq.

"Don't bother showering." Dan had been out of work for months and seemed glad to have an unemployed buddy. "Stuff your clothes in a bag, and get your butt down here."

Leo stared at Dan's angelic face. "I don't feel like it."

"Don't make me come up there."

"Dan, really."

"I've got everything we need." Dan patted the truck. "Tent, sleeping bags, food, beer. Get your hiking boots."

When the mailman stuffed letters in the slots below, Leo wondered if Heather wrote a note offering a clue as to where her head and especially her heart had gone. He desperately needed to view the future now that he didn't control it.

"I'm staying here in case Heather calls," Leo said.

"It's 2003, old man. She's got your cell number. I'm giving you five minutes to come down."

"Or what?"

"I'm coming up. I've never seen you so depressed."

"So?"

"It's creeping me out."

"Where are we going?"

Dan folded his arms across his chest as if he'd pulled off the biggest idea in his life. "Maine."

"All the way up there?"

"Nothing personal, but can you think of anyone who's going to miss us?"

Leo sunk on the windowsill.

"I think she misses you," Dan said, "but she can miss you in Maine too."

After driving until morning, they hiked through Baxter State Park for most of the day. Like some sort of aerobic-aromatherapy, the repetitive beat of the trail and the smell of the pines penetrated Leo's senses. He started feeling like his old self, or at least he no longer felt sorry for himself, although the heartache remained. In retrospect, he had stolen Heather from Dan, after Dan left her behind, and then later Leo took her for granted. Up until Heather said good-bye, Leo had relied on the fact that he had never left her, but she went and left him instead. This love business was crappy from all angles.

The men made camp for the night at the foot of Mt. Katahdin, the endpoint of the Appalachian Trail. Over an open fire, they cooked beans in the can and grilled steaks an inch thick. Dan pressed one cold bottle of beer after another into Leo's palm, which helped numb Leo's sore legs and feet. Not since spring training at Holy Cross had he worked this hard, but he was emotionally spent and took solace in the physical exhaustion.

"Tomorrow we're going up to the summit," Dan said.

"I figured that."

At dawn, they climbed the wooded trail until breaking into the sun-bleached terrain of Baxter Peak. The clouds passed low, actually below them at times, and for late May, the weather was unexpectedly cool and windy. Leo jumped on a lopsided boulder to scope out their path, and when the air cleared between cloud rushes, he spotted their destination on Pamola. A mile long ridge joined the barren summits, snaking up and down, with 2,000-foot sheer cliffs on either side. Hikers called this part of the trail "The Knife's Edge."

Leo watched Dan cap his canteen and snap it to his hip. En route to the summit, they hadn't spoken much. This was one of the joys of sharing space with Dan. The rest of the world filled Leo's day with phone calls, e-mails, and sound bites, most of which he immediately discarded. The silent trail allowed time for him to think, and the quiet filled him in an astounding way. He wanted more of this soulful emptiness. *Was there a place where life remained empty for long stretches of time and every action boiled down to a sharp mind and utmost self-reliance?*

"You ready?" Dan asked.

"Right behind you."

Leo allowed Dan about a ten-foot lead. Dan's steps appeared as confident as ever, and below them, the lush pine forests of Maine swept over the valley, leaving ice blue ponds like rain puddles.

About a half mile into it, the trail narrowed to less than eighteen inches. The cliffs fell away with jagged rocks that waited to shred them up on the way down in the unlikelihood they survived the fall. Leo shuddered with momentary thoughts of stumbling.

"Take cover," Dan announced.

Leo turned to see a cloud bearing down. The rolling gray mass appeared to carry more weight than gaseous water. It sped right for them, as if it might knock them aside or, maybe if they were lucky, pick them up and carry them aloft.

"Get down," Dan said.

Feeling the cold edge of the leading winds, Leo crouched to the trail. He gripped a protruding rock, as Dan vanished in the mist.

The cloud dampened Leo's hair, and tiny hailstones danced on the nearby rocks. His heart beat faster. Swimming in a cloud, he thought of what Heather might say if he died, and in a flash he considered his life in general—what he'd done and what he'd accomplished. Had it amounted to all that much?

"Leo?" Inside the cloud, Dan's voice no longer echoed.

"I'm here."

"This is crazy."

"Yes."

"You OK?" Dan asked.

Raising his face, Leo let the water bathe his skin. He stuck out his tongue and tasted rain.

"Leo?"

"I'm OK."

Like granules of sugar sifting down from the heavens, the hail came faster. Some of it melted right away; some lingered on the stones. It pricked the thin skin covering Leo's eyes and, as he lowered his head again, the back of his neck.

"Dan? I should've mentioned Heather sooner."

"Is she all right?"

"She's fine. It's me."

"What's wrong with you?"

"I should've cleared things way back when."

"Cleared what?"

"You know. Dating her in the first place."

Dan gathered a few seconds of thought. "Geezuz, that was so long ago I can't remember."

Leo still refused the initial truth. He had wanted Heather at first, not because she was free, but because she still loved Dan. He hadn't named those feelings until they sailed in a cloud 5,000 feet above the earth. "I should've talked to you."

"I would have asked you not to date her," Dan said.

"I know."

"And then she'd never find out that she loved you."

"It's not that simple."

"You make everything complicated. This is the way it is. No harm done."

Leo recalled the teenager who rescued him from a wicked hazing at Holy Cross. All heart, Dan was. Dan had no fear of the future or repercussion for any of his actions.

"What makes you the expert, eh?" Leo asked.

"I'm a pro. Don't you notice the ladies eyeing me?"

Leo saw his buddy emerging in the mist.

"When we get back, you're going to propose to Heather again," Dan said. "That's what I would do."

As the sun burned off the remaining fog, Dan's full form returned to view. He sat cross-legged on the trail eating a granola bar and drinking water, as if snacking in the clouds was part of his daily ritual.

"That was cool," Dan said. "I've never done that before."

"We've done some neat things, you and I." Leo sat down on the trail. "Thanks for taking me up here."

Dan swigged his canteen and looked up at the sky. "Man, it's beautiful up here."

Leo opened his canteen and drank. He would offer a treasure in return for Dan's friendship, to really give it justice. "What are you doing when we get back? Have you thought about it?"

"Actually, I've given it a lot of thought."

"Have you made up your mind?"

"I wasn't sure until just now."

"What is it?" Leo asked.

"I'm joining the Marines."

"No, really."

"I'm going over to fight."

"Are the Marines going to take your bum knee?"

Dan kicked out his leg. "I can do everything with this but break an open field tackle. I can kick terrorist butt."

"Kick terrorist butt, eh?"

"You want to join me?"

Leo studied his friend, who was sitting closer than he thought. "You need my help?"

"I'm going with or without you?"

"You're serious, aren't you." Leo thought to dissuade his friend, but instead saw the beauty of his simple plan. It would be easy to pick up and leave. As an active duty soldier, BCM would hold his job, and Heather? She would see him anew and recognize his commitment. Something both he and Dan lacked waited for them overseas. By sheer instinct, his friend seemed to know this. Was Dan smarter than he ever imagined?

Dan reached out his hand. "Come with me?"

Leo followed his gut, instead of his head. One more time, for the first honest time, they could prove each other's worth, side by side. It was an alarming and exciting proposal, without rules and apologies. Perfect. He wouldn't be the first person to go to war to find his missing self.

"Are you coming?" Dan asked.

Leo watched his friend rise and tower over the landscape. Dan seemed taller than Mt. Katahdin. Leo reached out and clasped Dan's hand.

◆

On the outskirts of Fallujah, they dug trenches between the railroad beds to guard the passing trains. Several of the stones used to support the tracks had been mounded in a ring around Dan's foxhole. He waited and watched, his rifle leaning against an olive green sandbag that padded his foxhole. Stuffing a sandbag required little effort in Iraq. It was a country of dust and sweat, and like most other soldiers, he hadn't showered in a week. Why bother? The clean didn't last but an hour.

For the most part, life had prepared Dan for military service. Sports training, especially in college, exposed him to long hours of physical labor, working through pain, and the meaning of teamwork and discipline. Civil service taught him about following rules, blind repetition, and an absurd chain of command that defied logic yet spawned confidence through creeping momentum. With this invaluable experience, the Marine Corps welcomed his arrival, and within weeks of reaching training camp, while some men harbored doubts, Dan considered a career in The Corps.

At the same time, Dan watched Leo wrestle with the new structure. Dan stuck close to him during training, and eventually Leo's old spark emerged. Leo needed to feel important, as if he was winning in most situations. Dan never noticed this so much, until boot camp stripped down each man and revealed his true nature. By the time they left for Iraq, Leo was their platoon leader, and his first assignment involved getting them to sign an American flag. They scribbled notes in the white bars, avoiding the red stripes. After the last man applied his signature, Leo folded up their colors and stowed it with their platoon supplies.

In quiet moments, Dan recalled the firefights near Baghdad and Fallujah. Tracers flew overhead and mortars exploded in stretches of pure insanity. He was rattled, especially since the war was supposed to be over by the time they arrived, but with rebels and old loyalists running amuck, Fallujah proved to be a real problem. You never knew where or when they might strike, partly because they barely held a plan from day to day, other than to kill the Americans, screw things up, and make U.S. soldiers appear at their worst both dead and alive. The enemy didn't know, or maybe they did, that the reports drifting ashore from home—the news media that never talked about the good deeds the Marines performed every day—wrought the most damage. Over time the platoon became deflated and then turned numb, merely thinking of ways to carry out orders and survive.

"Old man," Dan called over to the next foxhole.

Leo looked up from his notebook. Tucking his pen into his camouflage helmet, he spun his tan face toward Dan.

"Writing to Heather?" Dan asked.

"I took your advice. I'm going to let it stand."

When Leo had broken the news about enlisting, Dan was there. They were walking out of a tavern in Hamilton, just as Heather and her girlfriend were entering. Slipping aside, Dan watched from a distance. Heather latched onto Leo, her eyes tearing. Without making out the exact words, he knew that their stalemate was over. Joining the

Marines during wartime created the ultimate trump card to a lover's quarrel.

Spitting the grit from his lips, Dan watched Leo's head above the stones. "She's going to say yes. She'll set a date."

"You think?"

"I do."

"What makes you so sure?"

"You can lay odds on it. It's Heather. I've got a good feeling about it."

As Leo's eyes fixed on the horizon, Dan turned to see a local woman approaching their position. They were one half mile from the last structure in Fallujah, a place where insurgents had struck twice prior to derail the trains. There was no business in the world for a woman out here, especially wearing that god-awful black getup and head-dress in the midday sun.

"Stay alert," Leo commanded to the platoon.

The sun reflected pocket-sized mirages off the stones and the polished steel of the tracks. Raising his binoculars to his eyes, Dan watched the woman pace closer. She appeared to be alone and in her early twenties, but guessing a woman's age in this part of the world was dicey. After years of hard labor and many children, a woman often seemed ten or twenty years older than her American counterpart.

Dan looked back. "What do you think?"

As she moved within thirty yards, Leo fired a warning shot into the air.

In the most forward position, Dan heard snippets of the language that would always be indecipherable to him. He glanced at Leo who only shook his head. The others hunched in their foxholes, rifles at the ready, anticipating a blindside attack.

Five minutes later, she paced closer. Leo yelled and fired a second warning shot. She stopped again.

Dan scanned the expansive landscape—a terrain of sand berms and patchy weeds. No breeze, the afternoon was quiet and still, not a threat of rain for months to come. Looming in the distance were two burnt out hulks of SUVs from earlier assaults. If the enemy were coming by surprise, he would have to dig a tunnel from miles away.

The woman's voice sounded insistent, pleading. Dan rose from his foxhole, testing the air for enemy fire. He feathered his rifle trigger, wondering if his flak jacket and helmet would be enough to protect him. It was uncanny that his platoon had yet to suffer an injury. He stared the woman down. She might be a decoy or, even worse, wired to a bomb. There were no rules, only imagination to figure how crazy any single incident might get.

Digging into her wrap, she smiled, crooked teeth emerging in a dark face. Her eyes looked rich and brown like the sweet spot of a well-oiled baseball glove. Dan got the feeling that she was someone's mother. Mothers had to be the same all over the planet.

"What is it?" he asked in his best dialect.

Her arm shot forward, palm upward, fingers unfurling to reveal the grooved, fist-sized burl of a grenade.

"Geezuz." For a second, Dan lost his limited Iraqi vocabulary, and just as he was about to speak, a single bullet punched her chest.

She jerked backward and fell softly to the dust.

Dan hit the ground and covered up, waiting for a firefight that never began. From where he lay, he noticed the pin still threading the grenade.

The woman moaned and rolled onto her back. How many people she must have seen fall this way, but did she think that one day it would be her? In this crazy bombed-out town, perhaps this was her way of speeding life to its inevitable conclusion.

Dan rushed to assess her injuries. Leo came quickly from behind. Tripp with the field bag followed. Cruz got on the radio and called in for support. Now, they were field medics instead of guards, kneeling on the burning hot rocks in hell's notion of a struggle for freedom.

"What is she saying?" Dan asked.

"I couldn't hear her." Leo turned to Cruz. "You better get them here fast."

As her breathing became spotty, Dan helped to apply a dressing below her left shoulder. A lung had collapsed. They heard the telltale hissing through her chest. It was all so absurd. They couldn't pull back a woman's dress to see the damage, the locals taking it as an extreme insult, but even with the heavy material and the gauze, Dan noticed blood seeping up from the dressing and between his fingers. They were losing her. She stopped talking.

"What did she say?" Dan asked.

"I couldn't hear her," Leo said. "I didn't know."

"Geezuz. What was she doing out here?"

When Leo finally looked up, Dan knew that his best friend had fired the fatal shot. It was like Leo's face was coming apart.

"What did she want?" Dan asked.

Leo glanced at the grenade, which sat amid the harmless stones. "A trade."

"A trade?"

"She wanted to trade it for food."

At camp, in the temporary structure that barracked hundreds of soldiers, the platoon quietly read mail or lay on cots. It was only one hundred degrees outside, and the fiberglass roof partially diffused the sun. The sun in Iraq could never be tamed.

Leo stared at the long horizon, wondering how this place could be connected to any spot on the planet that he knew. It didn't matter to him that the CO had cleared the shooting and wrote it up as an accident. Sure, that was how it happened. Everyone said so, but his heart pumped to a different beat, and his conscience ached for a sin that had no penance. Leo began to see the world differently or at least the way it always existed. Dan was a person who saw a dangerous world and people who needed to be protected. Leo saw the same world and people who needed to be punished.

The platoon sat at picnic tables beneath camouflage netting, eating a dinner of powdered slop that they'd rehydrated with bottled water. Dan noted how their rifles had become extensions of their anatomy. Cruz kept his between his legs and poking in the air at an angle. Like most everyone else, Tripp and Emerson just leaned theirs by their sides. They had transformed into reactive machines. All the things that their boot camp sergeant said they would do, they had done, more so than in their wildest dreams.

Leo ate his gruel in short order, collected his rifle, and retreated into the barracks. The platoon, Dan especially, noticed that Leo kept to himself in the weeks following the Fallujah train tracks incident. It was strange. As a unit, they'd fired too many rounds to count, killing an uncertain number of Iraqis, but when a soldier mentioned "the shooting," everyone knew that he meant the Iraqi woman, and that single bullet from Leo's rifle. They all felt his anguish. When you lived and slept with the same men, when you killed with them, when you might be killed at any moment beside them, you knew what the others were thinking. Each man knew he might have squeezed the trigger and shot that poor woman. Each was grateful he hadn't.

Tonight Dan went after Leo in the barracks, and he found him hunched over a handheld computer, watching a video message from Heather. From across the room, Dan saw where this was headed. He walked over and snatched the device from Leo's grasp.

"Hey," Leo said, "Give that back."

Ignoring him, Dan strutted outside beneath the netting. Other soldiers filled the patio, and a handful of CO's bunched at a corner table.

Hearing Leo coming from behind, Dan held the computer screen in the air. "Look what I have everyone."

"Cut it out, Dan."

Dan curled the computer to his chest and gave Leo a friendly thump with his fist. "Big news, guys. Gather round."

Many of the soldiers left their seats to view the tiny screen. Dan queued the message, pumping up the volume as loud as he could. Heather appeared in a sexy black dress with her hair done up and wearing makeup.

"Oh, Mama," Cruz said. "You left that piece of ass at home?"

A few more Marines layered saucy, well-meaning compliments upon Leo's girlfriend. If you wanted to insult a man out here, you called him a coward, and no one ever did that, because cowards and heroes bled the same.

"Sssh!" Dan said.

They listened to Heather talk. She held up an oversized calendar board. One day was circled in black, and the following Saturday was circled in red.

"This is the day you're coming home," she said. "And this is the day I picked for our wedding. Does that answer your question?"

A cheer rose from the platoon, which swept through the diners outside. Pretty soon the Marines were barking their approval, and the CO's stood and applauded. It was as if they were all getting married next year.

For the first time in too long, Dan saw Leo's expression turn up—the edge of his grief dissipate if only for a moment. Dan pulled out his camera and snapped a picture. "Heather's getting that one."

◆

At a checkpoint outside Fallujah, Leo's platoon worked the snaking course of concertina wire designed to disable approaching vehicles. With residents trying to get home after the latest flare-up, traffic backed up along the highway nicknamed "Iraqi I-10." Leo scanned the long line of war-torn people. Coveted possessions bulged from the open windows of compact cars and over the rails of donkey carts. How was this different than any other war migration? Iraqis probably hoped that the Americans, Al-Queida, and the assassins from Iran, Syria, and Saudi Arabia would disappear with a single breeze, so that they might resume the less lofty pursuits of baking bread and prayer without collecting bullets in their skulls.

Until that day arrived, Leo and his crew owned the pleasure of picking through Fallujah's residents one at a time on the highway. If a renegade car approached the checkpoint, Leo's orders involved firing warning shots, followed by rounds to disable the engine. Heavier ammunition, such as grenade launchers, cued for the event when approaching vehicles needed further persuasion.

Leo saw Dan speaking to a member of the Iraq Civil Defense Corp. For two weeks, three ICDC members accompanied their platoon on detail. The Pentagon believed that rebels and old loyalists would be less likely to shoot at units that contained some of their own countrymen. Leo saw no evidence of this. Last week, a unit outside of Najaf had gunned down an approaching SUV that refused to stop. The driver had emptied an AK-47 toward the checkpoint guards who ducked in their foxholes for cover. No one at the scene noticed the driver scanning the guards for nationality.

Dan walked toward Leo, shaking his head. "I keep telling them to let the driver open the doors of the car for inspection. I mean, they want to do the right thing, but this is going to take forever."

"When they're on their own, they can do it any way they like," Leo said. "For now, be patient. They'll get it."

As the rest the platoon manned their posts, Leo and Dan stood near the Hummers with the grenade launchers. The trouble with checkpoint duty wasn't the danger as much as the complacency, which led to outright boredom. Twice the day before, Leo reprimanded Cruz for getting closer than he needed. It was true that everyone looked tired and benign.

Letting his rifle fall to his side, Leo took out a towelette to clean his face and hands. "You want one? I got a fresh batch from Heather yesterday."

"Maybe later." Dan scanned the cars. At work or play, dirt never seemed to bother him. "At least, we're not standing out in the sun doing nothing."

"Hey you know, I was thinking."

"Oh no."

"Listen to me. I was thinking about, after this is over, what we could do."

"I thought you were going back to Blake, Cauthen, Marzipan or whatever."

"Maglione."

"Yeah, right, whatever."

"I was thinking about that gym. I could look into it and stake you the money, become a partner."

"You pulling my bad leg?"

"I owe you, brother."

"Owe me for what?"

"It's not only that. I want to help you."

Dan studied him for a while, before his trademark grin assumed his face. He slapped Leo on the shoulder hard enough to send a shock along Leo's spine.

"Hey, old man." Dan took a couple of steps back toward the point. He paused to catch Leo's eyes. "You're going to make a good father some day."

"Screw you."

As Leo headed for the command point, he noticed the lead car stall just shy of the search area. It was a gold Subaru, and the driver wasn't getting out.

Dan waved Leo off. "I'll take care of this."

The ICDC men slunk toward the idling Subaru and exchanged words with the driver, eventually coaxing him from the car. Immediately, the ICDC men began opening the doors.

"No, no." Dan paced closer. "Let him do it. The slightest thing throws you guys off."

From a distance, Leo locked onto the driver's face. The man stood to the side with his hands in the air. He wore a simple white garment and sandals. At first, Leo didn't recognize him so calm and subdued. No, when he saw this man the last time, he and Leo were delivering supplies and apologies to the family of the woman he'd accidentally shot and killed. The visit was strictly against orders, but thinking it might help make amends and ease Leo's conscience, Dan had convinced Leo to come along. It wound up being a disaster, and to get out alive, they needed to turn their rifles on the neighborhood. If not for Cruz's deft driving of the Hummer, they might have made a perfect front page story for the *LA* or *New York Times*, strung up on a bridge trestle, minus their heads.

At once, Leo and the dead woman's father recognized each other. From yards away, civilizations and language barriers between them, they read each other's mind.

"Dan!" Leo aimed his rifle, but Dan was already in his sightlines. "Take cover!"

Dan glanced back at Leo.

The driver stood within a few feet of Dan, and when the vest packed with explosives and ball bearings detonated, it sent forth a blast that both blinded Leo and knocked him off his feet. The helpless feeling and the snapshot of Dan glancing backward would be permanently imprinted on his mind.

When he regained his senses, Leo felt searing pain in his thigh and legs, certain he was bleeding. Organized chaos swirled about him, and the uninjured Iraqis near the head of the line had abandoned their cars and wagons. With thick black petroleum flames braiding into the sky, the Subaru burned out of control.

Cruz was ahead of the others. "Fuckers!"

Leo breathed heavily, fighting to regain his feet.

"You OK?" Henderson crawled from his foxhole.

Leo had taken flak in both legs but needed to find Dan. Gripping onto Henderson's leg, Leo hoisted himself upward.

"Stay down, man," Henderson said, gripping Leo's shoulder.

Leo stumbled forward, spotting Dan's beautiful arm only yards from his position. He saw his wristwatch and hand, the whole arm, untouched but no longer connected. The madness of the mind searched for solace in spite of the facts. Leo limped further. God, maybe this was the extent of the damage. In fractions of a second, Leo figured out how Dan might carry on without an arm. He patched together an entire lifetime.

When Leo spotted another arm, his knees gave way.

Henderson eased him to the ground. "Man, don't do this."

Leo saw Henderson look ahead. He heard Henderson cursing. They both saw the same thing. An ICDC man lay dead and burning, decapitated from the explosion. They spotted another writhing in pain, and more parts of brother Dan.

"Shit, man. Shit." Henderson went on like that for a while.

Leo Harris pressed his face in the cursed, hot dust. His eyes were too dry to shed tears.

◆

On the transports that left nightly from Iraq, the coffins lined up inside the hull like jeweled monuments of red, white, and blue. Leo watched the honor guards and chaplains bestow their final blessings, a dedication to the stars and bars before the craft sealed its hatches and took flight.

Leo left his seat in the plane and moved among the fallen. He was barely able to walk, yet bore down on the pain. The Marines let him accompany Dan home. Unable to heal in time to be of any further use to The Corps, this was Leo's final duty.

On the outer row, Leo eyed his destination. Dan's coffin was easy to spot. The platoon had agreed to drape their colors over him. No one gave it a second thought. Their unique signatures and well wishes honored their first fallen brother in a new way.

Lying down beside his oldest and only friend in the world, Leo listened to the huge jet engines hum outside the craft. Foreign air whooshed beneath the hull, but his spirit remained grounded.

He pressed his hand to the spot on the flag that bore Dan's name. It read "Semper Fi" above his signature. Dan was the best damn team player Leo had ever met.

"I'm sorry, Dan. I'm sorry for everything."

Satellites, Cigarettes, and Whiskey

On a cold winter night after the decade of war and sex and the following decade of booze and drugs and the next decade of money and power, I came into my own as a writer. I'd grown up on authors like Hemingway and Dickens—travelers, adventurers, first class showmen who knew the value of their deeds, if not the weight of their words. I was almost thirty years old, too young for the 60's summer of love, too poor for the 70's summer of drugs, and too unconnected for the 80's summer of greed. It was the 90s, a throwaway decade in American history, years filled with angst, confusion, and irrational pursuits of wealth and fame. Just as deluded as the next person, I believed that I could make it as a novelist, but I still felt removed from the crowd, as if no one else harbored unfulfilled dreams.

Seated in an East Village nightclub, I waited for my next lukewarm mug of beer between sets from a popular New Jersey cover band. I'd quit cigarettes and whiskey, but as I inhaled the secondhand smoke that enveloped me like a comforting blanket, the jury was still out on my abstinence. I was caught in the in-betweens, having just exited a long-term relationship with an extended blonde headache who could blow my mind beneath the sheets while twisting it each second above them. Every time we touched the mattress, I felt as if I'd reached base safely, no danger unless I wandered too far away.

I'd met Trish while working for NASA, designing satellites that flew to Mars in preparation for an eventual landing on the red planet. Trish worked in the clean room where they assembled spacecrafts prior to testing. She had haunting eyes and curves that the white jumper could not hide. Studying her shape from the two-story overlook into the clean room, I watched her reading satellite design schematics while studying her grad school chemistry homework. The male technicians eyed her without shame, but whenever I visited the floor to spot-check the progress of my latest designs, I determined to play it cool. The room smelled like the inside of a brand new TV set just unwrapped from the bag—plastic, silicone, leaded solder points catalyzing the senses. I methodically toured the twenty-foot manmade constellations that hung from the ceiling in silver, gold, and platinum. As technicians peppered me with questions about circuitry placement and wiring, I told stories of launches gone awry and the day Challenger exploded over Kennedy Space Center like a star-crossed supernova. I avoided Trish. She was a mystical tome that you shouldn't approach yet promised wonderment for the risk. My aloofness toward her, she confessed over bedroom hits of Jack Daniels and ciga-rettes, hardened her resolve to get my attention. In her eyes, I was the head geek of the clean room.

Satellites, Cigarettes, and Whiskey

And I was an aspiring novelist, scribbling ideas and sentences into journals, waiting for a break that might never come. As the band tuned for their final set, I rose from my barstool in Rick's East Side Rock'o'Rama to find the men's room. In Manhattan, you can locate the men's room by the odor of evergreen scented urine, but inside Rick's, I already knew the spot. As a way to coast the in-betweens of my life, as a sure method of avoiding the blank pages to fill, I wasted Saturday nights in this dump, helping the band set up and break down for the 11 pm showcase. I was moonlighting, paid with the promise of free beer and killing time. In many ways, it was the best and worst job I ever had.

The band's lead singer was a girl named Lisa who wore spandex and a big ponytail and mimicked the better singers on the circuit. She sounded fine, but the group was destined for no more than weddings and junior proms. During our rickety van ride into the city, the group talked of disbanding, as if separating and reforming else-where might improve their mediocre talents. I thought about quitting too, considering an end to my writing aspirations. I wasn't practicing my craft regularly any long-er, and as I stood at the urinal, my father's recent words echoed in my mind: "You don't have enough experience to be a novelist."

Returning to the bar at the back of the club, I caught a glimpse of a blonde working the foosball table with a Puerto Rican guy who wore enough gold medals to open his own devotional stand. The blonde reminded me of Trish. In our final days, I'd been avoiding her, working late,

167

not returning her calls to my beeper. I was sick of her escalating moods, her orbits that denied all signals from Earth. On a rainy Monday evening, after she'd submitted her final chemistry thesis, I'd asked her to get out of my apartment. She expected a bottle of champagne and an all-nighter—a trivial argument exploding into broken glass, the smashing of dishes, and maybe the perforation of plaster with fists. Raised by an alcoholic mother and a father who managed crises like a blind fireman, every celebration was to be tempered with heartbreak. I popped a cork on a bottle of Moët and broke her heart for good. At that moment, I think she never loved me more, although lately I'd heard rumors that she was flirting with a biker gang during her first internship at a pharmaceutical corp. I guess she had more expansive dichotomies to explore.

Right now, a cute brunette with a small nose and short hair that spiked at the fringes sat on the barstool in front of my writing journal and foaming beer. She chatted with a dark-haired woman with slender hips and a belt made of chrome-plated chain. They both wore the black uniform that the 50's beatnik poets donned and Lou Reed made famous but likely stole from Andy Warhol. In the way women do, the pair leaned toward each other and spoke, fully focused on each other as if no one else in the joint existed. Men's eyes constantly roam the horizon, even when they aren't searching.

Reaching into the narrow space behind them, I snatched my journal and beer from the bar. The brunette didn't budge, but the dark-haired one shot me the oh-was-that-your-seat look with no intention of moving. Up close, the women were faux bohemian. Their clothes pretended to be purchased from the rag shop on Bonn Street but were uptown dress-down all the way to their designer boots. The brunette's jeweled Rolex was likely more expensive than my car, although none of this offended me. I felt more comfortable with phonies these days and their unabashed ability to skirt reality.

"Sorry," the brunette finally said.

Ignoring her apology, I bided my time, enduring the final set from the next backup players to the K.C. & The Sunshine Band reunion tour. Soon I would be loading drums and guitars into the van for a depressing trip through the Lincoln Tunnel where the hookers waited for a turn and, if traffic backed up, just a few encouraging words. On stage, the band broke into someone else's hit. I thought that Lisa's spandex outfit with the pink stripe racing up the thigh wasn't all that different than the hookers' getup by the tunnel.

Lamenting my denial of whiskey, I paced myself through a mug of beer. This was my version of being monastic—no smokes or hard liquor, no Trish, and no writing. If I eliminated every vice, I might tally the left-overs. *Maybe my father was right. Maybe there would be nothing to find—no wheat, all chaff.*

The dark-haired woman asked for a light. By habit, I still carried a book of matches, but I also carried my writing journal, and I didn't seem to use that either. Digging the matches from my pocket, I flipped them onto her lap.

"Thanks." Her voice trailed at the start and end of sentences, as if her words traveled from a far away place. It reminded me of the gravelly communications I had received from space. Waiting for the delay between transmissions afforded time to consider your words.

"You don't work on Wall Street, do you?" the dark-haired woman asked.

The brunette was just as lively, studying the notebook beneath my arm and the pen tucked in my ear. "Are you some type of reviewer?"

Funny, no one had ever confused me for a writer. I finished my beer and ordered a refill. "Actually I'm a rocket scientist." I often hid this information, certainly never phrased it this way. Even though I was entrenched in the business of spinning gyros and solar array deployments, I considered myself in transition. But where had my gumption for becoming a writer gone? I used to arrive at work early each morning, pretending to be absorbed in paperwork and calculations, instead working on my latest novel, but I did not believe in myself as an author, no courage to make the incredible leap of faith that I would take six years later—abandoning a six figure income, placing it all on the line, and "putting a bullet through the head of a brilliant career" as my boss would say. For now, my existence was just an elaborate sham. I hadn't yet realized that the fantasies and human insights, which would dominate my thinking over the next decade, stood just beyond the gossamer veil that kept people separated from their truths.

Satellites, Cigarettes, and Whiskey

But I wasn't the only one sending up smokescreens. Marcie, the dark-haired one, and Sheila, the brunette, were successful stockbrokers, but they weren't interested in stockbrokers, financial advisors, or anyone connected to their industry. We began rapping about the band and music in general. I'd made the mistake of expecting them to be vapid club girls, not successful women of their own mind. Expert tacticians, they avoided all the dumb questions and barroom feelers. Trish had taught me every one. Women ask if your girlfriend is waiting and if you just came from your job, assessing potential and income right from the start. Men size up breasts and hair. Men are stupid. Only by trudging through the landscape do men learn the terrain. Women already know the pitfalls and hairpin turns. Men live their lives with their eyes, but women somehow see better.

The band's set was loud and obnoxious. I felt loose and brave. With Trish in my rearview mirror for almost two months, I still expected to find her ranting at my apartment door with a shotgun or, even worse, a member of the Pagans biker gang, who was pumped up on her fairy tales of abuse and prepared to avenge them with the sharp edge of a switchblade. At one time, I worried about escape velocity and stress points on spacecraft that can barely manage their own weight within Earth's gravity, but Trish was a heavier load to bear, not to mention a schematic without a logical circuit. Even Einstein had no workable theories about crazy blondes, and it wasn't for a lack of hands-on experimentation.

For forty-five minutes, the women at the bar tag-teamed me in conversation. Just when I caught the vibe from one, the other stepped into the banter and took the lead. Messages transmitted between them like coded signals—curious eye movements, hand gestures, and indecipherable phrases. I was either tired or distracted, imagining their interest.

Marcie had painted her eyes Egyptian style, not overdone. To catch the effect, you needed to be as close as I was getting beneath the blare of the snare drum.

"Do you play an instrument?" she asked.

"Blues guitar, just for fun." I threw a shoulder toward the stage. "Not this stuff."

"We have a synthesizer back at our apartment," Sheila said.

"That's cool." I reduced my vocabulary, moderating my beer consumption. I was minutes from packing the van for the return trip to Jersey. "What type of synth do you have?"

Marcie stared at me over the edge of her gin and tonic. "We like to double team."

To this day, I swear they were talking about playing the keyboard at the same time. In my ignorance, I was the coolest customer on the planet. I doubt my eyes dilated in the slightest. "Great."

Marcie gave a slight head tilt, a private acknowledge-ment that I would never mistake in the future.

I was all reception, like the huge satellite dishes at Goddard Center on the coast of Maryland—ready, waiting for alien contact.

Satellites, Cigarettes, and Whiskey

As the band hit their finale, Sheila leaned over to whisper in Marcie's ear. This was my cue. They were doing one of two things: selecting who was going to give me their number or deciding how to ditch me. In my narrow perception of the future, no other option existed. Feigning no notice of the deliberating jury, I leaned over the bar and asked for a glass of water. At this very moment, my better manuscripts circulated Manhattan. *This town will judge me on all levels.* I prepared for rejection, sort of.

When the set broke, the houselights went up and x-rayed the haze of smoke and exhausted patrons. Marcie disappeared into the bathroom. Sheila threw her purse over her shoulder. "We have a place in Battery Park."

OK, it was Sheila. I felt an ancient cultural response. *Sheila wins. She chooses.* The American Indians operated like this. A man was much better off with a woman who selected him, not the other way around. History was littered with arranged couplings that were spurned by unreceptive women, spawning cataclysms from murder to all out warfare. I started thinking about Sheila in a less dangerous sense, how I might write her up in my journal: a bold and balanced chin, quick wit, sarcastic laughter, guarded yet open-minded, slender and agile arms like the flawless titanium controllers of an AS3000. After all the insanity with Trish, it felt so damned right for the evening to go down this way. Sheila told me she'd read *The World According to Garp* and cried when Jenny Fields screwed a dying soldier in the hospital without ever speaking to him. I realized that I better find my words, needing a semblance of vocabulary to evoke her imagination.

I told Lisa, because she was the only band member who wouldn't be angry with me for not helping them break down their equipment, that I was quitting the job for a more hopeful position. Lisa eyed Sheila and Marcie lingering by the door. During many egghead moments in the past, she'd caught me reading Stephen Hawkins at the bar between sets or sketching designs on a cocktail napkin. Her image of me suddenly shattered, I waved my journal in a grand good-bye gesture.

The taxi jittered downtown. Sitting between two slightly older but deliciously clean and attractive women in the back of a midnight cab ride through the city of blinding lights was enough inspiration for most men to write a book. A moment of perfect expectation arouse that I hoped would freeze in a holding pattern for hours like a flight into Kennedy International. Energy resonated between my shoulders and the person sitting beside me. Anything was possible. Hoping to cleanse my soul, I was jetting toward Sheila's downtown apartment. I fully expected Marcie to clear the runway.

Upon our arrival at the ladies' one bedroom place, Martinis were in order. Gin was distilled from juniper berries and smelled of the woods. Their apartment overlooked a forest of buildings, including a couple of towers that waited to collapse into oblivion on a day that changed everyone's life. No less irreversible, tonight's transformations were singular and private.

I threw my leather bomber jacket over the kitchen chair in the far corner and plopped into the middle of the couch near the door. Kicking off my shoes, I stretched and yawned like a lion amid the pride. Someone threw an R.E.M. CD in the player. Into fluted glasses with twisted fuchsia stems, Sheila poured the mother of all cocktails.

Her sandaled feet parked beside my socked feet. She had elegant, painted toes like fingers. Her breath was sweetmeat—gin and anticipation. My throat went dry. I needed to steal a kiss.

On the opposite side of me, Marcie took a seat. I counted three drinks on the coffee table. Three drinks? *Shit.* Somewhere I heard Trish laughing from inside a laboratory or around a campfire with the chrome of motorcycles reflecting in the flames. Several of my old writing journals and collector's editions of Faulkner's works had evacuated my apartment with Trish. One by one, she was ripping the pages from the stitched bindings and burning them in a campfire, or she sat locked inside a dim laboratory, feeding Faulkner to a Bunsen burner.

I leaned back against the velvet cushions. A Tarkay diptych spanned the wall—women in Victorian getup taking tea on a European veranda, women in the private space of other women and their words unrestrained.

"Tell me what it's like in space," Marcie began.

"It's a vacuum. It's terribly hot and cold, depending on the position of the sun." I thought about the ride home that I'd missed in the East Village and the lonely train ride that awaited me. The turning points in my life formed ugly constellations in my mind, and a pervasive sadness filled my heart. As crazy as it sounded, I'd wanted to work things out with Trish, but how could I be her savior when I couldn't even plot my own trajectory? As long as I could remember, I knew I wanted to be a writer, but instead I chased satellites across the heavens and the odd free-lance journalist assignment to nowhere. I sat with strange women in Battery Park in hopes of a relationship that was going nowhere. This night had to be the end of something.

Picking up my martini and swirling it beneath my nose, I decided to get drunk with a couple of classy women who felt that I was as safe as I imagined them to be, and then I would scramble through the frigid Manhattan streets for a ride home beneath the pitiless New York sunrise.

"I can't imagine what it would be like to circle the Earth," Sheila said.

"I used to dream about going into space," I said.

"Really?"

"I don't know anymore. It's anticlimactic. You work on the spacecraft. You're nervous at launch. You hope every critical piece initiates as designed and then sometimes they don't."

"What happens?" Leaning into me, Marcie put her hand upon my shoulder, getting comfortable like old friends do. The clock showed 2 am. Somewhere along the line, Sheila called me "rocket man," which was the dumbest of all clichés, but I forgave her.

"Batteries run out of power," I said. "Solar panels jam, programming goes haywire. All your plans go to hell. You're left with the drawing board, apologies, and the long faces of the guys in the clean room who'd believed for months that you would pull off the impossible."

Satellites, Cigarettes, and Whiskey

Steadily, the women interrogated me, rarely breaking from their line of questioning. They seemed to examine my word selection and tone, and hearing my voice in my ears, I became acutely aware of the structure of my sentences. Downing my drink, I shuffled to the bathroom by the front door to prepare my exit. One or both of the roommates were interested in me, maybe neither. It was too late to fumble for the answer and too early to wedge between friends. Gathering water into my open palms, I examined my face in the mirror. An unfamiliar reflection presented itself.

The living room was quiet. I heard the sound of the clock humming in the kitchen before I noticed the women on the couch. The couch faced away from the door, and when I entered the room, only the occasional sight of a foot rose above either end of the arched back. The women's shoes were discarded, their calves bare, and they were silent, until Marcie crackled a moan that weakened a young man's knees.

The rocket scientist in the room finally understood, sort of. The girls were friendly, very friendly—most friendly with each other. I heard Marcie again. I didn't need a roadmap, just one to steer clear. *Hey, had they thought I left already?*

Across the room lay my leather bomber jacket on the kitchen chair. I really liked that coat and it was freezing outside, otherwise I might have slipped out the door unnoticed and left the girls to their pleasure. Sauntering across the apartment to grab my jacket, I planned to toss it over my shoulder like James Dean cutting corners through a porno film lot. I planned to salute the pair, Paul Newman style, hardly a gesture, as if I'd seen this couch show a million times prior and was unfazed.

The girls were stripped naked, down in the muff, their clothes tossed on the floor. Stutter-stepping, I caught a glimpse of what I might never come across again, not in any deep space exploration for certain, not within a million miles of the exotic territories that I explored for a living.

Sheila raised her head. "Aren't you joining us?"

Three years later, this moment returned to me as I submitted my resignation and received a lecture from my boss, who was livid over my "irresponsible" decision to pursue my dreams. I recalled Marcie and Sheila who dropped the veil to share their own experience. Thoughtful and intelligent, they operated by a completely different set of precepts, and in the next forty-eight hours, they would learn more about me than Trish had in months or my boss had in years of living alongside me. I was governed by angst, fear, and a set of rules that no longer worked and likely never did. That night in Battery Park, I rewrote my operating instructions. I started looking up, down, and behind, less often straight ahead like most others did. People rarely understood what lurked behind their own veils, much less someone else's. As a writer, it was my job to unearth the details and report on them, to handle the mirror that let us view ourselves clearly.

Sheila laughed, knowing the steps toward liberation better than I did. Marcie, behaving more like Cleopatra by the minute, beckoned with a curled finger in case I lost my nerve. Although in part I was merely a tool for their recreation, I entered the late night engagement primarily out of curiosity and with the naiveté and stamina of youth, the way an aspiring novelist entered his first attempt, determined to distill thought and emotion into being. The second time involved affirmation, and the following times invoked the hard combinations, but again, I was a writer of limited experience, as my father had so assuredly stated many years ago. Today I explore new landscapes for clues, up to my hips or my eyeballs, depending on the horizon in sight. Occasionally I come across a piece of slick technology that seems sexy, but there is nothing as appealing as a blank page and a fresh idea.

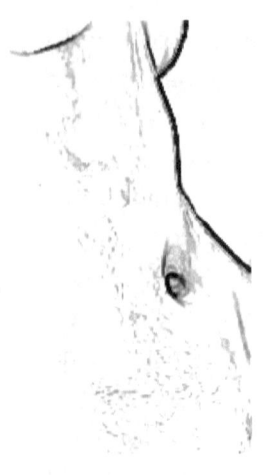

Complete Exposure

When I first saw my naked wife, she was standing at the stovetop flipping boneless chicken breasts. Our five-year-old son, Rudy, sat at the table, brushing a red crayon across a page in a coloring book. He was naked like his mother.

He raised his bright face. "We're going natural, Daddy."

My wife transferred the chicken to a plate, her pink breasts jiggling with the motion. Smoke slipped past the range hood and kissed the ceiling. Garlic and rosemary tinged the air. "We've given up clothes," Laura said.

"Angela and Pam are natural too." Rudy was referring to his unclothed sisters shuffling about the living room.

"Don't worry, Michael," Laura said. "I haven't abandoned diapers. The girls are keeping those."

All four of them seemed content, but I was seven moons removed from it. A computer virus at work had thrown my client base into disarray and my reputation into serious doubt. I didn't know the full extent of the damage, but when I came home, I wanted warm comfort and a cold cocktail, not my family roaming the house like a coed locker room.

"Think of all the money we'll save." Laura stopped fussing at the stove and came to greet me. "It's very green, ecologically smart."

Any other night but this one, I thought. Don't get me wrong, I adored Laura, and three kids later, she held up great, clothed or unclothed. Sometimes I wondered, as less of my hair grew and more of my gut showed, if she still found me attractive, if she still recognized the man who years ago stumbled into her apartment with a prayer and an apology, but I never wanted her to pause and take notice. Her love—the way she cast it toward me—flowed like a dream, and even raising the question might jar her awake.

"You don't look so good," she said. "Have a rough day?"

My tongue jammed like a knotted drawstring.

"Want to join us?" Reaching for my belt, she was far too casual for my mood. "It'd be fun."

This had to be a joke. Laura was not foreign to pulling off surprises, but with the kids *au naturel*, I started to wonder if this was the antithesis of a joke, where I was the only funny part.

I went upstairs and sat on the edge of the bed. After pulling off my black loafers and socks, I tossed them in a heap with my suit. With a swing of my outstretched foot, the bedroom door slammed shut. I hadn't meant to close it so hard, but it rattled the picture frames on the wall with a metallic sound like a prison cell door crashing into position, and then it was quiet and serene. Only the sound of my breathing reminded me that I was alive. A faint echo of other prisoners, other men, emanated from distant cells.

The clanking of dishes snapped me out of a trance. I jumped up and took a quick shower to wash away the day's bad karma, and somewhere between the shampoo and the spiraling tornado of soap, I decided to play along. I put on a pair of boxer shorts and returned to the kitchen.

"Is that the least you can muster," Laura said, twirling lettuce in the salad spinner. Her skin glowed beneath the glaring kitchen halogens. Her hair tousled with the cranking of her arm.

Laura in motion, I thought. She had the randomness of a fly on a fruit bowl. Knowing I would never be bored, I'd married her because of this, but here was my next thought: She had set up a web cam, and we were going live on the Internet for 99 cents per minute to whatever freak desired a bare glimpse of suburbia.

"Is this a forever-change?" I asked.

"What's a forever-change?"

A forever-change was an event like losing your job. That hadn't exactly happened to me, but maybe it wasn't a bad idea to salvage what we could. In this economical age when people put everything—every slice of time, every body function, and every two-bit scrap of leftover junk—up for sale on eBay and the pornographic versions of eBay, I found myself scanning the kitchen for hidden cameras. *Nothing.*

"What's the matter, Michael?" she asked.

The kids moved happily about the den. Rudy searched a box of crayons for the perfect shade of red, and as an episode of *Sesame Street* went ignored on the TV, Angela and Pam built a lopsided tower of blocks. Everything appeared regular, sans clothes. Why did their nakedness matter? For most of my bachelorhood, I had tried to strip women of their clothes and get out while they were still undressed. A significant part of my married life involved creating time for nude encounters with my spouse, but I couldn't believe my mind. I was considering how to beg Laura to get dressed.

The doorbell rang, and before I flexed a finger, Laura was at the front door and signing for a package. The deliveryman—a husky guy in a brown uniform—stood inches away from my wife, almost hovering. *These are the images in life that placard the inner walls of your thoughts.* She must be getting even with me for something I'd done a long time ago.

The conversation at the door was snappy. It had been raining for days, and Laura and the deliveryman quipped about the monsoon weather. This guy was a real pro. What was his day like? Along his route, he probably came upon plenty of odd situations, but his eyes never strayed from Laura's face, not for a second.

As she shut the door, Laura spotted me paralyzed near the kitchen table. A new expression had no doubt welled up from the nightmare of my day. I was the man of a thousand troubled faces.

"He didn't notice your outfit," I said.

She shrugged her shoulders. "He was here earlier today."

◆

In the morning, I carried my anxiety to work, where I spent hours apologizing to coworkers and every client in my e-mail address book who'd received a pornographic message from me. Even my mother received one. The way a computer virus penetrated undetected and performed its scheduled misdeeds, it was a skilled agent of espionage. I had no clue who'd saddled me with the MILF-o-gram virus, only plenty of evidence that I had passed it along by the feedback burning up the company help line. For many quiet and successful years, I worked at School Stuff, Inc., a grade school supply outfit in San Diego. My clients were teachers and principals scattered about the country. It was pointless to e-mail them and warn them not to open my previous message. It would be too late by then. Imagine the phone calls I was forced to make: "So, ah, Principal Davis, ah, have you read your e-mail lately?"

I made a priority calling list, but before I connected with most clients, they had already viewed a full-screen video of a housewife doggy-styling the plumber on the kitchen floor. My boss, Chip Apostulous, who had thinning peach-fuzzed hair, ranted like a child with a dirty vocabulary, and somehow his foul language didn't matter. Chip said I was "skating on thin ice," "screwing the pooch," and "fucking up big time." All the standard clichés shot from his mouth. So many idioms existed for the same sentiment: You are in the deepest trouble of your life without being killed or maimed.

Sitting in Chip's office, I countered his threats with my best excuses. I made apologies for my apologies, but nothing seemed to click with reality. The entire time I thought of my wife. One hint of her new naked attitude, and everyone at School Stuff would cast the knowing eye. *Well, if this goes on at home, no wonder he's mailing porn all over the country.*

"It wasn't my fault." I unconsciously ground the rubber tip of a fresh No. 2 pencil into my palm. Since arriving at work, I had been chewing the inside of my mouth.

"Not my problem," Chip said.

"Maybe I can offer them some type of discount as an apology."

"That would come out of your pay, if…" Chip paused for that turn-of-the-corner that you never wanted to see in regard to your job. "…if you get another paycheck."

"You can't be serious. I've put in seven years here."

"Hey, Rome wasn't built in a day."

"What does that mean?" I felt the stranglehold of injustice. I was begging when I did not have to, and it still wasn't enough.

"It means that Rome took a long time to build and it burned in a single evening."

"Oh, man."

"Between you and me," Chip said. "I'm sure glad it wasn't my computer."

I took little solace in his flash of empathy. When I saw him do this to others in the past, I used to laugh, but he was insincere and unconcerned, playing a robot role in my surreal drama.

"It's the guys at the top," Chip said. "You know, it's out of my hands."

◆

When I parked in the driveway that evening, I was fully brain-fried, my boss' threats slipping though the sludge of my worries. I needed to cool out and build a plan to redeem myself, but as I rose from my metallic gray BMW, I spotted Laura's gorgeous rear end poking up from the tomato patch. Normally this sight pleased me, and in any other sequence, I might lose myself in the view. Some men were breast men. Others built fetishes around hair or feet. I was simple, a tried and true ass man, but at the moment, Laura's butt—sunburned and ripe as a tomato—emerged through the sprawling vegetable greenery. I watched her get up on her knees and wave hello. She was as naked as a squirrel.

The joke or the experiment—whatever her excuse— was over. Last night I had been too preoccupied to press her for answers. Tonight I saw only three solutions to the problem: admit defeat and join the lunacy, admit defeat and ignore the situation completely, or admit defeat and start an argument. Being married with a family, defeat was often part of the equation, no matter how I parsed it. My father used to say, "Defeat is the first stop on the road to change." My father said other things that didn't prove true over the long haul, like "When you got something good, stick with it," which didn't fully explain why he had never lived with us for more than a month or two in a single stretch. No way, I wasn't going to be a husband like him. I was going to face this issue head on, instead of ignoring it. Man, I needed a victory somewhere.

I stomped toward the garden. Our kids hopped nakedly through the sprinkler. We were a figment of an old hippie's imagination.

"Laura, you're not dressed."

"Yeah," she said, matter-of-factly.

Trouble in my life seemed to stack up like credit card bills. I hadn't told her yet about the MILF-o-gram business, and maybe this wasn't a good time to get into it. With little effort, I pictured her as the star of the next porn virus update. While we spoke, the local pervert was probably gathering video footage through the hedges.

"You're naked in the backyard," I said.

"It's our backyard."

"It's still outdoors, as in public nudity?"

"Don't get technical with me. I'm only gardening. I'm not flash-dancing the neighbors."

"Not yet."

"Michael, cut it out." My naked wife—the woman with the dirty knees and elbows and waving a hand shovel like a toddler at the beach—was telling me to "cut it out," to stop acting so immature. "Do you know what your problem is?"

"No, tell me."

"You're embarrassed of your body."

OK, I wasn't perfect, and I wasn't in as good shape as Laura. God bless her, but I worked every day for a living—sitting at a desk, filling out paperwork, and filing orders on commission. Who had time to exercise with a personal trainer or eat according to the USDA Food Pyramid? I was putting a normal American roof over our heads, which might be the next thing Laura jettisoned in favor of a log cabin or grass hut.

"You're crazy," I said. "What in hell drove you to become a nudist?"

"The word is *naturist*."

Ah-ha! She had been doing research. Laura never made a move without first ordering brochures and maps, without raiding the reference section of the library, or without running the Internet search engines to exhaustion. Her moves only *appeared* random. Would our next vacation involve a shady campground in the Arizona desert, with nude volleyball, naked disco, and me worrying about where to sit down?

"I'm going inside to get changed." Frustrated and angry, I stomped toward the house. My modesty, which I never imagined existed, became a giant weight on my con-science. Laura was free, naked, and loving, and I was nothing but denial. A million suffering men wept over the waste of it all.

◆

I poured myself a double martini, but a double martini is more like a quadruple something else or maybe even a sextuple. During that really big, fluted drink, I lost count of my intake and lay down on the bed in my boxer shorts and socks. Too drunk and overdressed to come to dinner, I stared at the ceiling and pondered deeply about where I'd gone wrong. This was the prelude to hopefully, vacuous sleep. It was, after all, why I ventured the double martini in the first place.

But I dreamt regardless. I dreamt of sheep, of sheering sheep and seeing them gather about the green hills of my neighborhood, even though my neighborhood was all townhouses, pavement, and little patches of lawn. I dreamt of sewing sweaters for the naked sheep out of their own wool and chasing them about the fields while trying to re-clothe them. It was hard to put a sweater on a sheep, even a wool sweater.

With the sound of the light switch clicking, I awoke, drenched in a pool of cool martini sweat.

Laura stood over me. "You look like you're going to puke."

She'd shaved her pubic hair completely. I wondered if this was part of the naturist code: to strip it all off, to come completely clean—a visual confession to the world, to reject the common veils and accept yourself as you were. How many people could do that? I couldn't. Part of Laura's new creed was very Zen, if you never had to leave the house. Was the hair on her head going next?

Soon I was splashing my face with cold water at the bathroom sink. I thought about other couples that had dramatic changes thrust on them, like one person going blind or brain dead or losing both limbs in a freak railway accident, but they held on to their sanity. Without as much as a hint from a friend or a notice in the mail, serious changes happened that laid waste to the dynamics of a relationship. It was akin to a sudden computer virus attack—something you never expected and completely unfair. The loss of clothing was a manageable disability. The loss of a job—I couldn't even put the possibility into words—seemed like a far greater tragedy, like a complete failure.

I found Laura on the corner of the bed, watching me recover from my martini-induced nightmare. Cross-legged, leaning back on one arm, she appeared as come-hither as I'd ever wanted, but I no longer understood what she wanted, since occasional nudity was my signal and constant nudity signaled my distress. Maybe Laura was right and I didn't like nakedness after all. I'd become too damned uptight, and I was unable to face it. Without a word, I bent over, kissed her forehead, and left.

I started to drive. Taking the BMW, I blew past the stone and wood-sided townhouses on our block, which were better than a lot of houses on other blocks. I needed elbow room, to get out in the open and properly bitch. A frisson of thought allowed me to understand why my father had disappeared for days on end: He wanted the decisions of his life to be only about him. As I tried to turn around the turnarounds in my life, the facts were hard to digest. I could have put down my foot. I could have screamed at Laura and laid down nasty crap that convinced her to get dressed. All of the time, people committed degrading acts in private, and it wasn't so terrible. Couples hung in there, creating something tolerable from outright insanity.

My car wheels turned with their own momentum. I was automatic driving. In truth, I owed Laura for every positive turn in my life. I was certain she knew this—one of those understandings that bridged the gap between a man and a woman. When she found me, I had been a complete bachelor or what a woman might call a total bum. After sleeping with women, I never called them back, and I knew this when I slept with them. I took jobs until I gathered enough cash to quit and drop the wad on a month-long jaunt in a warm coastal destination. On a trip like that, I cannot tell you what I did, except position for golf tee times and tee up the next woman. Who cared if she was young or old or single or married? My exit was my excuse to forget her. Nothing was permanent and the law was only a concept. Certainly people carried rules and principles they kept neatly folded inside their conscience until the moment they needed to break them. By keeping no rules, I broke no rules. I drank the truth and they sucked a tit of lies. Living in the moment was my currency. Comings and goings were my art. Without question, this made me good at sizing up people. At a random gathering, I spotted the pretenders: the hard-edged sensitive chicks, the phony tough-talk guys, and the clay-footed libertarians. Sucking the tit of lies. Self-delusion brought a man back to where he started better than a thousand dollar GPS system.

But I never saw Laura coming, and she had appeared so easy to figure out. On the San Francisco waterfront, I'd met her at a book fair, not far from where the harbor seals stunk up the piers. That was my sign: The good and the ugly often appeared side by side. She was sexy, sweet, and smart in the most natural of ways, which was why her recent naturist routine didn't really surprise me. She liked her body and mine. There was a truth in her that I could not resist, except for my need to control the endgame, because the endgame always arrived out of the blue.

Six months after Laura and I met—longer than I'd spent with any woman on the planet, other than my mother—I searched for the first signs of trouble. It unnerved me that she could shift my attention by doing something amazing. She would uncover a group of dinner recipes that actually needed to be burnt to taste good or dress in pages of Shakespeare's sonnets and recite them until they were all gone. Who else thought of stuff like that? I feared she was better at endgames than I was and that the end might come flying at me like when the carnival knife thrower suddenly missed, which in the knife thrower's case was not missing but hitting his assistant pinned to the spinning wheel.

I was spinning, and after lining up a job in New York, I crept from her Clayton Street apartment at dawn. My belongings were stuffed in two suitcases, along with a ticket for a San Francisco Airport departure. Traveling light by habit, I was used to moving between women and jobs like a bag lady with access to a hot shower, and the return to a familiar routine invigorated my senses. I didn't own a car. Not even my name was on the apartment lease. I took the $500 that she stashed in the drawer for emergencies and covered up the blank spot with the note cards I'd given her on her birthday just last weekend. On other occasions, I had walked away with cash and hearts. No promises of anything to anyone. *Leave first. Exit on a high note. No one else but heaven needs to know.*

◆

Another workday passed before my bosses at School Stuff thought differently about second chances for second-degree crimes in which I had been unwittingly implicated. The perception, which was more potent than the truth, was that I had randomly porn-SPAMed the grade school community across the United States of America. It was a computer hacker's *coup de grâce*. True, my wife was touring the neighborhood in her birthday suit, most recently during a naked coffee klatch with, Rita, her girlfriend down the block. However, the right press coverage might transform me into a combination of the Janet Jackson boob flash and Larry Flint. My boss didn't need that kind of media exposure, and only days after "the computer incident" as it was being called, I was summoned to Chip's office for another meeting.

"We've had time to evaluate our position." Chip refused to look me squarely in the eye, even though he spoke with the full force of management. All signs point-ed to the notion that he was about to erase the company blemish by deleting *me* from the payroll. "We don't feel that you can stay on with us any longer."

I was probably the first official job casualty of SPAM. I held my tongue. It was pointless to defend myself once fate had already mowed me down in the street. The only task that remained was to numerate my injuries.

"We're extending your pay and benefits to the end of the month," Chip said.

It was the 23rd day of June. *Wonderful, a day of severance pay for every year I'd spent at the company. Thanks for the generosity, Chip.* "This is entirely unfair."

"I know where you're going with this." Chip held up a hand. "Don't even think about coming after us."

"I have rights."

"Rights?" Chip tried not to laugh. "Do you really think you'd win after the way you soiled our reputation?"

I considered how corporations behaved. They might hire a detective to dig up information and make me look as guilty as possible. The way Laura was dressed lately, they would only need to show up in my neighborhood with a cell phone camera. As Chip might say, I was "totally screwed."

This put me in a stormy summertime mood, although I managed to leave the office without cursing out the boss and telling the blabbermouth in the next cubicle to seal the infernal hole in his face. Privately I conjured nicknames for everyone that I could mix and match from the MILF-o-gram virus soundtrack. Several times, I had watched the video in disbelief, not that I wasn't familiar with the various acts portrayed in grainy pictures and uneven sound, but that housewife was a real dirty talker. She put the F back in pornography. The joke, which wasn't so funny from where I stood, was that I knew school-teachers. I'd dated many before Laura. All day long, they maintained their composure while little Janie sneezed in their faces and little Johnny bit their ankles, and then they let off steam in private in ways that you might find shocking but I came to respect. There were several teachers, I bet, who appreciated my unintentionally delivered e-mail video.

Regardless, I left without laying the MILF-o-gram's greatest quotes on the heads of my coworkers. Believe it or not, I still needed these people for job references. As I walked toward the exit for the last time, my so-called peers stared at me over their cubicle walls. They judged and juried me as if they had never once done anything shady, even Betsy who got drunk at the Christmas party last year and offered me a blowjob that I didn't accept. Maybe they only saw shades of their potential unfortunate selves, but instead of sorting out that noise, I took the next best course of action. I raced home to pick the fight with my wife that I couldn't get started earlier in the week.

◆

Just before lunchtime, I arrived at our townhouse and discovered Laura conducting a naked Tai Chi session in the living room. The neighborhood wives were lined up, arms and legs spread, doing the Peng Ching. At one time, I thought it might be cool to come home and find a house full of naked women. It was not cool. I conjured visions of having to apologize to people on my entire block as well.

"What are you doing here?" Laura screamed, breaking from her peaceful center.

The Peng Ching was sometimes called the "ward off" stance, and I was being warded off my living room carpet by a gang of disturbed and offended women. The disturbed wives were covering up in a stance that I didn't think came from the ancient Tai Chi scrolls, and the offended wives, the ones more comfortable with their nudity like Laura, yelled at me, hurling pillows and then books like ninja stars. I was the only clothed person in the room, and I barely escaped without being mauled. As if in an earthquake drill, our kids scattered underfoot, diving beneath the coffee table and stairwell. I thought Tai Chi was about health and serenity. This was obviously the western version of the art form.

I retreated to the bedroom, even though there seemed to be no safe place for me. At times like this, a man wondered if he should pack up and leave. What use was I to anyone around here? In the course of two days, I had inadvertently offended my clients, my coworkers, and the co-inhabitants of my block. I no longer had a job to support my family. I even got dressed in the morning. Where did I fit in?

Laura came upstairs, her anger as bare as the rest of her. "Is it too much trouble to call when you are arriving unexpectedly?"

"Sorry."

"You should be, and why aren't you at the office?"

For what seemed like forever, I had been hoping to tell her about the completely funny incident at work and how it had blown over after a day or so of porn talk and panicked thoughts, but now the joke had become me. I had actually been fired. Could I erase the truth of it from my face? I did all that I could to cover up. "Why are you always undressed?"

"Not that again."

"Is nude Tai Chi even allowed?"

"Please, Michael."

"Are you going nude to the PTA meeting tomorrow?"

"Maybe I will." A naked woman threw so many dynamics at a man that it resembled standing in traffic. Even an angry naked woman captured him staring in the headlights.

"You're kidding, right?" I asked.

"Who's kidding?"

As I studied my beautiful, crazy, naked wife, I recalled that this was my fight to pick. "Tell me, really, why no clothes?" I began speaking in a pseudo Tai Chi language, standing firm and strong, knees slightly bent, pointing my finger at her samurai style. I was mixing all the martial arts at once. "You need... clothes."

Laura glared at me. It wasn't a committed glare, just a standoffish rampart, the palms of her hands open and white.

"Tell me," I continued. "You have any idea how upsetting surprise nudity can be? What it can do to people... all across the county? And, and careers even? You understand how nudity can ruin a career?"

Laura's shoulders dropped. "What's the matter, honey?"

197

Oh, how I hated her patronizing, compassionate tone of voice when I most needed it. I felt my heart climbing in my chest. This was how it happened, I thought. A man got fired, came home from work, found the whole neighborhood naked, and had a massive heart attack on the spot.

"OK," Laura said, "you're upset."

"You think?"

"This is not about me yelling at you downstairs, is it?"

Then and there, I should have told her about getting fired. She was going to find out soon enough. For everything it was worth, I should have taken her in my arms and held her and cried over the inequity and then made love to her as the naked neighborhood collected themselves in the living room below, but I was a man used to being in control, guiding my own fate, and discarding what I no longer needed. Today, the world was out of order.

"What the hell are you doing with me?" I had meant to pose my words as a rhetorical question, but they came out mean and nasty, because I felt the same. In hindsight, it sounded as if I had said, "What am I doing with you?"

"Talk to me," she said.

Incapable of replying in an intelligent fashion, I collapsed on the end of the bed. My house, wife, and kids—all of it—tugged at me, strangled me. I was scared and didn't like the feeling. The pull for me to escape was as strong as my self-loathing for thinking that I might actually leave. Any second, she was going to see it clearly.

"What if I'd just stayed on that plane all those years back?" I said. "I wouldn't be trouble for anybody. There'd be nothing to worry about."

Laura mirrored my fear, revealing a whole set of emotions that I'd spent a marriage trying not to tease to the surface. "What are you saying, Michael?"

I turned away from her. "Forget about it."

"What are you saying?"

I grew silent.

◆

Alone after our blowout, I fell into a mongrel state of supreme bastardness. I started screaming to myself, kicking the clothes and furniture in our bedroom, terrorizing the remaining occupants of our home. It was a full-grown toddler shit fit. Man, I hated myself. I smashed a vase, because I'd seen it done on TV and thought it would feel good. It did not feel good. Crashing, shattering, the broken vase left a fist-sized hole in the wall and bits of ceramic and plaster in the DVD player grille that would likely never sweep clean if it didn't kill the machine altogether.

But who really cared about the DVD player or the hole in the wall? I struggled mightily with an old sin that I never forgave myself for committing. It was an ugly gem from ten years in the past—a past that haunted the inside of the San Francisco Airport terminal. At weak moments, it stabbed at me during fitful nights of sleep, and I was thinking of it now. Once I had been confident and cocky, no need for thunder to strike the target. Laura's stolen heart and cash had been tucked in my pocket, and through the oversized airport terminal windows, the trees waggled in the breeze, cheering me onward. I felt the push, the adrenaline of new adventure that numbed the senses. On the runway, the plane cued like a rocket ship, its long silver body gleaming in the sun. Overhead, the destination board read: Clean Getaway – ON TIME.

I took it.

In flight, I watched the city by the bay grow small and stupid below me. I pictured tiny Laura going through her morning routine in her apartment: first seeing no coffee in the maker, my jacket missing from the hook, followed by the empty hangers in the closet, the holes in the CD rack, and the final discovery that I'd stolen her money. Except for the cash, the stuff I took was of no real concern. I stole the money not because I needed it, but rather this singular act closed the deal, no turning back.

The road ahead was a libertine's dream, which I had successfully navigated on numerous occasions. It led to other women and more easy times, but the finality of leaving Laura filled me with an unexpected grief. I mean, I was the one who had left. I was the one not coming back, but somehow it felt as if Laura had suddenly left me, as if I'd gotten a tap on the shoulder mid-flight: *Excuse me, sir, the captain wants to speak with you. There's been a terrible accident. We're so sorry. Will there be people waiting for you at the airport?*

In the back of the plane, the emptiness overwhelmed me, and dropping my face in my hands, I wept. *I am needy and shameful, and she sees me for what I really am.*

During the layover in Chicago, I walked the terminal like a homeless man, mumbling to myself, garnering worried glances from fellow travelers. Stumbling into the nondenominational chapel, I confessed my sins with nothing but a strange mosaic of vague icons drawing witness. *I love her, and she is alive and broken from me, further than half the country away.*

With the Midwestern sun cutting severe angles through the airport double-glass windows, I caught a glimpse of myself—a shocking reflection that lined up my past lives with laser clarity. Images of my father appeared within those outlines. In my lifelong quest to avoid him— to avoid being anything to anyone in particular—I had become my father. I was unworthy of Laura's favor, but that was the only grace that I craved, that would mend my soul.

At the ticketing counter, I abandoned my plans and bought a boarding pass for a return flight. By now, I was sure that I had stunned Laura into despising me, flipped her love on its head, and I was doing what? Returning to San Francisco?

At the San Francisco airport, I scraped together quarters for taxi fare. My plan involved handing back her money, taking rejection in receipt, and disappearing from her life like a blessing tailor-made by me for her. *She has already called her girlfriends. Like witches, they are evoking my name in incantations. "He is a boy," they are saying, "not a man." They are making sacrifices, running scissors and steak knives through our photographs together.*

At her doorstep, I clutched my suitcases like a man returning from war, hoping for proof that the Dear John letter was a mistake—the Dear John letter that I had crafted with my exit but disavowed as I returned her money and offered a lame apology. At first, I saw the face that I had refashioned with selfishness and the confusion of my unscheduled arrival, *but my God, against all odds she still loves me.*

◆

At the PTA meeting, I banked once again on Laura's affection. Days of grim job applications and interviews had passed. There were a few prospects, but nothing very attractive. Laura and I hadn't spoken since the argument, and the silence burned a hole through my confidence. Without her support, everything I did lost its touch and feel.

Alone in the Jefferson Elementary School boys' room, I made myself right with my decision. Part of me wanted to skip the scandalous event, gather the required bail money, and prepare my excuses: *She hasn't been well, officer. Please excuse her appearance. She's been under stress since I lost my job. You know, it might be a very late case of post partum depression. Other wives have committed post partum murders. A little nudity isn't so terrible, is it?* When the time came, I thought, I should layoff the murder examples.

First my shirt came off. It was a blue cotton oxford that Laura had given me last Christmas. I folded it neatly. Next came my pants, a gray twill pair that Laura had said made me look sexy. I zipped my remaining clothes into a gym bag, slipped out of my loafers, and acclimated my bare feet to the cool floor. It was five minutes to nine in the evening. If my girl was going all the way down the naturist path like a monkey in a, well, monkey suit, I would do the same. I kept thinking that this was where the "for better or for worse" rubber met the road. Later she would have to deal with my tales of woe and unemployment, but right now she needed to know that I could forgive her for anything, as she had always done for me.

I looked at myself in the half height mirror beside the half height urinals. The only blessing was that no children attended a PTA meeting. The last thing my family needed was child endangerment charges. Public exposure and social humiliation would be enough in the short term. Somehow, we would navigate those minefields.

The hallway received my nakedness without regard, because the hallway was empty. I thought about how I looked. I was not Brad Pitt, but who really was? Up close, I bet Brad Pitt wasn't Brad Pitt. Only a few steps away from the school theater, I moved closer to where the PTA meetings were held. I slipped inside the room crammed with hundreds of concerned parents, and took a seat in the last row.

It felt cold to be naked in an auditorium. Goose pimples emerged on my skin, and my nipples shrunk up. Everything shrunk up smaller than actual size, but amazingly, no one noticed me, except for someone's grandmother across the aisle who occasionally winked in my direction.

I placed my gym bag over my lap. I must have looked like either an anxious streaker or a man in a Speedo at the

PTA meeting. Either character fit the occasion like an oil executive at a global warming conference.

Where in hell is Laura?

I was relieved to see her face among the last to enter the theater, and I rose to my feet.

The crowd gasped. A collective wind-sucking ripped across the room. Without warning, the head of the magazine drive committee fainted on the dais, and her body draped over the table like a fallen curtain. I had hoped for better commentary. A crescendo of whispers accumulated into a rumble of voices. *All those mouths shooting off at once, who can make sense of it?*

Laura's eyes were wide, but her face was proud and smiling and all my worries vanished. She still loved me as much as on the day I darkened her doorway in San Francisco with the windows and doors to my soul thrown wide open.

With no doubt in her mind, amid the PTA's most infamous gathering, Laura calmly strolled to my side and embraced me. Sure, there was going to be a price for this stunt and the kind of public chatter that lasts a lifetime, but it was worth it as Laura's arms encircled me and confirmed the attachments that were more viable than any of the nonsense that divided us. I held her tight, and I felt my bare skin against the pleats of her skirt and the buttons of her blouse.

Christopher Klim is the author/journalist of several books, including the satires *Jesus Lives in Trenton* and *The Winners Circle*. His other books include *Idiot!*, *Everything Burns*, *Write to Publish*, and the *Firecracker Jones* series. *True Surrealism* gathers his stories into a complete set for the first time. He is the executive editor of *Best New Writing* and the chair of the Eric Hoffer Award for books and prose.

Praise for Klim's previous novels:

Idiot! (2007)
"Klim challenges us, not only changing genres, but by offering a unique small town portrait..."
–The Midwest Book Review (Editor's Choice)

The Winners Circle (2006)
"Clever and Funny." **–Publishers Weekly**
"Sure to cinch Klim's place among the top humor novelists..." **–Book Reporter**

Everything Burns (2004)
"Absorbing reading. ... grabs readers with a solid plot."
–Booklist

Jesus Lives in Trenton (2002)
"Summer recommended reading." **–NPR Radio**